Walking Trees

Mary Qwell

DEDICATION

This book is for my family who have to listen to all my
ideas and give me so much encouragement.

A bit about me? My name is Diana but often called Di. I am now retired from paid work so have time to bring out all these stories that have been bouncing around in my head for so many years. I have three grown up children and one granddaughter. I have always had a pet dog and until recently I had a horse who took up most of my leisure time. I worked in many fields locally in retail, office work and with an advice service. I specialized in Debt management for the most part and then went on to work in welfare rights. I have a very supportive husband who jokes that one day I will be able to keep him in a manner to which he could easily become accustomed. At least I think he is joking. I do hope you enjoy this book and if you have a look at the back pages, once you have read the story you can see how to contact me. I would love to hear from you.

ACKNOWLEDGMENTS

To John for all your help in proof reading. My Sister-in-law Lesley who read the book and gave her approval. To all the members of Waveney Authors Group for your help and encouragement .

Walking Trees

Chapter 1

'That damned girl will be the death of me, I swear I'll swing for her. Up and down, up and down like a nodding sodding dog.'

Esme and Gris looked at each other quizzically, Nodding dog?

'Oh, you know those stupid things people used to have on their car dash boards. Dogs that nod.'

The girls still looked Puzzled.

'What the hell am I explaining myself to you for? Bloody curtsying every, bloody time she came in the bloody room. She was in and out of that room, must have been a hundred times. My knees are killing me now. The bitch enjoyed it, watching me bobbing up and down demeaning myself.'

The Wicked step mother was definitely in one of her rages and at times like this most of the people in Hardwick Manor thought it would be prudent to get out of the way. Griselda, however thought it was high time that her mother accepted the situation. She and Esme were about to be married. Cinderella had introduced them to two very respectable gentlemen who were to become husbands to the so called 'Ugly sisters.'

'We could have gone to the work room to look at the samples. You insisted on staying in the parlour.'
The slap Gris received was not entirely out of the blue but sudden enough for her not to take avoiding action. Oh yes, her Mother was in a rage and it would be likely to last for several days.

'Get out, you stupid girls, if your feet weren't so big, we would all be living in the Palace by now, one of you married to the Prince. Get out, Get out. And send in my maid'.
As the girls left the room they bumped into Rose, the unfortunate maid.

'Sorry, Rose but she wants you and you can probably tell what sort of mood she is in'. Gris told the girl while holding her inflamed cheek and trying not to cry.

'All part of the job, Miss Esme,' answered Rose as she braced herself to enter the room.

'Thing is Gris, those shoes were never going to fit us, were they? There were Ella's, made for her by the Fairy Godmother. So why is Mum so angry with us? It's not our fault. And even if one of us had got to be a princess she'd still have to curtsey.'

'I know Esme, it's in the story and that's the way it had to be. Mum has held a grudge for hundreds of years' now. I for one, am getting a bit fed up with her rages.'
The girls went up to their shared suite and decided to sort out their wardrobes. That always cheered them up. When Ella was still there, she would receive all those cast off's

She would take them to her work room and remake them into fantastic clothes for herself. Esme and Gris had always admired the result. So it was, that they had asked Cinderella to design their wedding dresses.

Ella was also making them some lovely clothes for their trousseaux, so the girls decided to make room for them, by getting rid of some of last year's items which were out of fashion now.

'So, what do we do with all these?' Gris asked as they surveyed the pile of rejected dresses, blouses, jeans, shoes and jumpers. Remember when we always use to give our cast off's to Ella but now, she has better clothes than us. Although she could never use our shoes.' She giggled

'I'm not sure, said Esme 'they just used to somehow get to Ella's workroom. I suppose we need to call someone.'

'Well we'll just have Buttons take them away and he can do whatever he likes with them.'
Esme went to the door and called out
"BUUUUUTTONNNNNS"

'Oh, for God's sake Esme, when will you learn to ring the bell and Buttons will come. You don't have to screech like that'.

'Oh yeah' she giggled.

'Coooee! girlies, what can Buttons do for you today?' Esme and Gris looked at each other and then stared at Buttons in pure disbelief. How dare he be so forward and informal with them? He never has been before, always treated them with disdainful respect. Ella was his favourite and he showed it whenever he could.

'I know what you are thinking, dear hearts, and no I haven't lost my mind. I am leaving this place. I am going later today. Ella has offered me a job with her at the Palace. Her very own Personal Private Secretary. P.P.S for short, same as Dan is for the Prince. I'm so excited and OHHH I will be able to see Dan every day. He is such a hunk.'

'Dandini?' Squeaked both the girls, in unison. 'You, and Dandini?'

'Yes, me and Dan and why not, may I ask? Oh, you didn't think he was of your persuasion, did you? Oh, dear me, no he is most definitely a queen, gay boy, poofter, call it what you will, but he and I are an item. I guess you want me to get rid of this pile of old clothes, do you? I'll go get a big basket for them dear hearts. Oh, by the way, your Mother has just reduced Rose to tears'.

When Buttons flounced out of the room, the girls continued to stare after him. Then they both sat down on their beds in shock.

'Dandini and Buttons? Buttons and Dandini? Yee Gods!'

'Well, I always knew about Buttons being gay, but would never have suspected it of Dandini.' Esme laughed.

'Oh, good grief, I always knew about Dandini, but I just didn't see it in Buttons. I think it will take a bit of getting used to, them being together, still you know what they say?' Gris answered

'No, what do they say?'

'Um, don't know'. Both girls giggled and waited for Buttons to collect their old clothes.

'By the way, what does Buttons do with all our old stuff?' Esme pondered.

'Probably sells it all on the market. I don't really care so long as we don't have to carry it anywhere'

Baron Hardwick arrived home to find his wife in a real state of apoplexy. She was also very drunk.

'Oh dear, you have been to visit Cinderella again, haven't you?'

'YESH!' came the drunken reply.

'My dear, when will you realise that you no longer need to be angry that she married the Prince?'

'It'sh in the shtory, in't it?'

'Yes, but the story ended hundreds of years ago. You really must get this into your head. You are becoming a total embarrassment. I really cannot allow this to go on.'

'And what do you think you're going to do about it?' she screamed at the Baron.

'Think you're so bloody clever now, don't you? It was your daughter that caught the Prince and inveigled him into marriage. My own sweet girls get the left overs.'

'Left overs, indeed. If MY daughter had not introduced them to their husbands to be, just how do you think they would ever have got married?'

'Oh, yes because she is so bloody beautiful. The bitch.'

'Bloody Hell woman I have just about had enough of this, you have got to stop being so bloody angry or face the consequences.'

'Consequences? OOOHHHH and what do you mean by that? Never mind, you're too gutless to do anything about it and I WILL continue to be angry because I hate the bitch. And I refuse to let my girls marry second rate gentlemen. Not a title between them. They should at least marry Dukes. The wedding is off. I will find suitable husbands for them both'.

As the Wicked step mother staggered from the room, the baron poured himself a stiff drink, settled in his favourite chair, brooding over the behaviour of his wife. She really has gone too far, and he knows he is becoming a joke among the younger courtiers.   He heard the main door slam, got up from his chair and looking out of the window he saw his wife make unsteady progress across the sweeping lawns towards the Enchanted Woods.

'Well maybe a bit of fresh air will do her good' he thought.

'Papa, what just happened? Mother said she was going to cancel the wedding, she is on her way to the palace now.' Esme screeched as the girls burst into the room.

'Oh God! I suppose we had better go and look for her. Just ring Ella and warn her, will you?'

'I think she is already in with the Queen. Is she drunk? She looked a bit unsteady on her feet when she burst into the palace, she was screaming obscenities at everyone.' said Ella when Esme phoned her on her mobile.

'I think so and, in a rage of course, you know what she's like Ella. Perhaps you had better go to the Queen's apartments and head her off at the pass so to speak.'

'You watch too many westerns, Esme, you know that don't you. Alright, I'm on my way, I'll let you know what happens.' Tell Papa not to worry, I have it covered this end.'

Chapter 2

As Ella walked into the Queen's apartments her senses caught the cloying smell of gin. If the Wicked step mother had got as far as the Queen's apartments, she wasn't there now. Oh well. Ella thought. There isn't much I can do about it.

'Hello, my dear. Would you like some of my special juniper tea'?

'Thank you, but no, I would really rather a nice cup of hot breakfast tea if some can be rustled up'.

'Pity, but of course you can.'
By magic a pot of strong tea was placed in front of Ella.

'Now Cinderella, I need to speak to you about your sisters' wedding'.

'Oh dear, I usually only get called Cinderella when I have done something wrong, is there anything the matter?' Trying to sound normal so as not to upset the Queen. When really, she wanted to get out and look for her step mother.

'No, no I just had a rather terse visit from your step Mother who told me in no uncertain terms that the wedding has been canceled'.

'Good heavens, whatever has got into her now? That woman is becoming too much, I know poor Father is at the end of his tether with her. Did you happen to notice which way she went?'

'She was drunk as a lord, my dear, and I should know one when I see one, so to speak. But I don't think Juniper tea is her tipple though, judging by the smell of her breath.' The Queen shuddered at the memory. 'She really is too much, we must put a stop to her behaving like this'.

Ella could see that the Queen had already lost interest in the subject and was looking for another cup of her Juniper tea. Ella wondered just how many bottles of gin the Queen consumed each day, but all her royal duties were carried out and she could function in a perfectly reasonable manner, most of the time. That is, apart from when she wandered around the palace in a drunken haze. Ella decided that it was really none of her business. In all the time, she had known the Queen, it had never been any different. She knew the King disapproved of the Queen's lifestyle. But he considered himself above such petty matters. In the main, just so long as he was never embarrassed by the Queen or her behaviour, he didn't see any reason to intervene. If the Queen wished to pretend her cup was full of tea instead of gin, then surely that was her business.

Ella's mother on the other hand was a real worry. The woman was a laughing stock and she knew that the whole of Fairy land considered her a joke. How, she wondered, could she be curtailed?

Dandini entered the salon and bowed to both the Queen and Ella.

'Prince charming requests the pleasure of Princess Cinderella's company for supper   in the high tower, Madam'

The Queen giggled. 'How very formal, Dan. Well off you go my dear, you must not keep your husband waiting. He must always be obeyed you know.'

Ella thought she caught a smattering of resentment in her mother in law's words as she rose from her chair, curtsied to the Queen and left the room followed by Dandini.

'I believe Buttons is to join the household?'

'Yes, Dan he will be moving into the same servant's block as your apartment. He is to be my Personal Private Secretary, same standing as yours for the Prince'.

Dan tried to cover up his smile under his formality, but Ella could see how pleased he was.

'I know you two will get along splendidly'.

'Yes Madam, I think we might. Oh, by the way your step Mother has left the palace and was last seen heading for the Enchanted Woods.' Dan told her knowing she was wanting to ask if the woman was still about.

'You've heard I suppose?' Ella asked as she entered the high tower dining room.

'Oh, yes. So has Father and he is not pleased. This wedding is just a few weeks away and the invitations went out months ago. Oh God, the whole of Fairy land will be laughing at him now.'

'I can't say I blame him for being upset. Whatever has got into the woman Charley?'

Charley had long ago decided that Charming was not really an appropriate name for a Prince. He had adopted Charles as his name. He considered that Fairy tales left a lot to be desired once the story had finished, and their lives carried on. Now in the 21st century, although they still lived in Fairy -tale land the boundaries between the two worlds had been broken down. Of the many differences, he thought the fact that they were immortal was the main one and they could no longer be expected to stay in the story.

He had central heating installed in the palace, instead of coaches for everyday travel he had a fleet of autocars. There was a swimming pool and a Gym, the children were taught all the modern subjects in schools which even included science. An unnecessary subject for Fairy 's perhaps because if they needed anything, they just used permitted magic to make or get it. But the Prince knew it was important that his children knew about the Upworld and that integration was inevitable. They now dressed in modern clothing, much of it designed by Ella.

Her skills at designing and making clothes had emerged at the time of the story. Those designer clothes she had revamped. This, she had built into a thriving business. Taking in unwanted clothes and designing newer, more up to date items. As the years passed her business grew until she employed thousands of fairies. She even sold some of her re-made clothes to

Upworlders and was breaking into the fashion world. In turn, the Fairy world could purchase designer clothes from there. Yes, barriers were breaking down all the time.

But right now, there was a big problem to sort out.

The King entered, and both Ella and Charley rose from their chairs.

'Well what are we going to do about this situation? I can't just cancel the wedding the invitations went out months ago and people, fairies, Goblins, imps, trolls, and every kind of Fairy tale creature are coming here to celebrate. We have spent millions on this wedding and we are likely to upset a lot of beings.'

'Please highness, don't take it all to seriously she will calm down when the drink wears off. The girls are of age and able to decide for themselves if and who they marry. They won't let her spoil it.'

'Your Father should have taken that woman in hand many years ago. She is a total nightmare. No other Fairy land has to put up with this constant barrage of hate for centuries after the story.' Ella thought this was a bit unfair as there were many examples of anger in the other stories.

'Unfortunately, she is in our story and as such we have to put up with her.' Charles told him.

Ella was in a turmoil. She agreed with the King that her step mother was uncontrollable but couldn't help feeling that if the King had not been so reticent about her and Charles marrying, they could have had the state wedding and this one would be a much smaller affair.

But the King had not approved of their liaison and had down played their wedding. After so many years he had to admit that Charles and Ella had a good marriage and were a credit to the land. So, he had agreed to this state occasion for her sisters.

The Queen put on her outdoor cloak and went for a walk about. She still gave the impression of being under the influence of the gin, but as soon as she was clear of the palace, she stood upright and walked briskly towards the Enchanted Wood. She knew that going for a ramble was expected of her. She always did when there was any kind of upset, saying that she could not cope. But with a purpose she now went to visit her old friend. Deep in the woods was a hidden door. It was set into a large shrub. The only people that could see it and knew about it were the occupant of the residence, the Queen and one other. As she approached, the door opened and the Fairy Godmother stood in the entrance.

'I have been expecting you, my dear.'

'You've heard?'

'Of course, but what to do about it?

'She has to be stopped, sooner than later. She must learn that things have changed, and we are no longer story book characters. I need to find her and try to talk to her properly.'

'Not something I can do, she has always hated me, but you can. You have the spells. Come in I have some more drops for you.'

The drops she was talking about were ones the Queen took daily to immunize herself from the alcohol in the gin. The gin she drank in ever increasing amounts, so she could live in the palace and go anywhere un-noticed. Everyone thought she was permanently drunk but because of the drops she was always stone cold sober. For many years now, the Fairy Godmother and the Queen had been working on a plan to reunite her with her only love. The marriage to the King, an arranged communion had never been happy for her. She had left her lover behind at the marriage and was working on a way to get back with him. His letters arrived at the Fairy Godmother's house and were so full of love and endearment it broke her heart for them to be parted.

'Are we ready for me to go?'

'He is waiting for you. You can go as soon as this wedding is over.'

'We need to find the bitch first. She must be encouraged? Would that be an appropriate word? To change her mind. There is no reason for him to come here without that ceremony. I could cheerfully kill her for this. If she stops the wedding, I will never have another chance to get back to my own story.'

'Don't upset yourself dear, we simply have to find a way to negate her objection.'

'I'll see if I can find her and talk to her. But it's no good appealing to her better nature, I'm not sure she has one. The time lapse spell still has a few hours on it, I may be able to find her before I am missed at the palace.'

'Good luck with that, I'll know if you've managed to find her or change her mind,'

For an elderly looking Fairy , the Queen could move with alarming speed. Her search would not last long at that rate.

Chapter 3

The Wicked step mother awoke with the morning dew on her. She was wet through, cold and her old bones ached from lying on the ground. Her head was banging and her throat dry. The day was bright, warm and sunny, and she was lying in a shaft of sunlight, but she took no joy from it. She knew she would have to find her way home but didn't recognize this part of the Enchanted Woods. The very trees had an ominous look and it seemed as if they were trying to grab at her clothing.

She felt fear, which intrigued her. So that's what she had been inflicting on others all her devilish life. How interesting. She liked the power that gave her and vowed to illicit more fear in all those she hated. Starting with that bitch Cinderella. Standing up and shaking off the fear, with her confidence returning she puzzled which way to go. So full was the canopy, suddenly, above her that the day had been blotted out, the sunlight had all but disappeared and the darkness crept into her very soul.

The bird song she heard on awakening was gone, all was silent. She tried calling out but heard nothing. Had deafness overcome her? She took a step and broke a twig which snapped. She heard that. She tried calling again but no sound emitted from her. Beginning to get annoyed she picked a path and walked determinedly towards she knew not what. The trees were closing in on her. The path that had been wide, closed over making her squeeze through small gaps. 'Not this way then' she said silently and tried to retrace her steps, but there was no path to follow. Turning she found the trees even closer and moving nearer still. Her feet refused to move. It was as if she had been nailed to the ground. The more she tried to pick up her feet the more she struggled.

Roots were growing from her feet anchoring her to the very spot. She began to feel very frightened. 'There is magic here.' She said but still no sound came. She screamed but again it was silent. As the first tree hugged her in an evil cuddle of death, she knew there was no way out of this. A second tree closed in on her and she felt the breath being squeezed out of her. Panicking now she tried to breath but found no space in her lungs to take in air.

The trees were pushing in on her crushing her ribs which broke under the pressure. Excruciating pain shot through her body. With each bone crushing and grinding she was now very frightened. How would this end? She had no magic, which had been another source of annoyance all her life. Living on her wits she reasoned she must find a way out of this situation. She was not supposed to die after all she was an immortal. She was evil and destined to bring misery and pain to all for eternity. That was her purpose. She confidently reasoned that this must just be a lesson she must learn.

All stories had a moral and this would be hers. But as the trees closed in even more, she began to realise the end had come. She was going to die here. Real fear enveloped her now. This is where it all ends for her and struggle as she might, the trees held her in their wicked grip, pressing, squeezing, breaking her. Grinding her bones to powder. With one last breath she screamed again and this time she heard her own ugly gurgling, dying gasp.

At the Parliamentary conference of Dukes, Viscounts, Earls, Marquises and Barons along with the King and Charles, the discussion on a parliament in the style of the Upworld Country England was ending. The long hard preparations were coming to fruition. Many years ago, the King had decided he wanted to make his story world into a democracy. The two houses of parliament had now been built and were ready for a grand opening. There would be places in there for all ranks of Lords and they would have a vote on each new law. But the lower house would be elected members of the parliament. Each town or village would have a representative. Everyone over a certain age would have a chance to decide who their representative was. The voting slips were in the process of being printed. The news coverage was full of proposed candidates telling the general population what they would do to make life better for all. Some were all for bringing back magic to general use. Some wanted taxes to be raised, to allow for paid health care. The Magic proposers said this would be an unnecessary expense. The King was amazed at how many things his subjects wanted to make law. The conference ended, and the Lords went back to their respective houses to prepare for the new lives they would live. This was the biggest disruption to the lives of the Fairy world in living memory. And as they live forever the King reasoned, that was a very long time.

 The King and Charles conferred after that last meeting.

'A good few years work there. It's been in my mind for a long while.'

'Just heads of state with no power, sounds good to me. State openings, foreign visits and no big decisions to make? A whole new world of royalty.'

'Yes, it would take a lot of the pressure off. Any changes in law would be democratically decided. We would have no say. It's called politics, and of all the Upworld political methods, I think democracy is the best bet. It gives everyone the right to have a say in the laws of the land. People power.'

'You've done well to get the Lords to agree to all this. They are real sticklers for tradition, but you've brought them round.'

'Well, maybe we've outlived our purpose. Maybe we shouldn't be rulers as such in this age but as you say, heads of state with no political power. Well that's that for now shall we go for a ride on such a lovely day?'

 Horse riding was sure to calm the King's nerves, it brought him solace from the cares and often fraught running of the palace and the whole land. He enjoyed

21

the company of his son when riding out. It had been three days now since that stupid woman had stomped out of the palace. Nothing had been heard either from her or about her since that day. Things were calming down and he hoped she was just hiding somewhere and feeling highly embarrassed. He would have a few things to say to her when she did finally put in an appearance, meanwhile just enjoy the peace and quiet of the lovely country side, his beloved horse, and the company of his son. His pride and joy. They did get on well and he knew Charles was ready to take on greater duties. Charles, for his part was trying to ease his Father's burden and worked hard to take some of the strain.

But this ride was not to be the comfort the King had hoped. Soon into the ride one of the outriders had approached at breakneck speed.

'Sir's, there something up ahead that looks like a body. It seems to have no bones and is flattened out.'

When they had reached the wide sunny clearing, they saw the flattened corpse of the Wicked step mother. The King ordered that no one approach the body and sent one of the servants back to the palace immediately to notify the police. The three-day search for her was over. She was found.

Chapter 4

The Police arrived and took over the clearing in the woods. A white tent was erected, and forensic officers were examining the body before the Wicked step mother, Madeline Hardwick, could be moved.

'So, D.C.I. Crumb, do we know how she died yet?' the King asked as the Detective Chief Inspector was asked to sit in the presence of his majesty.

'Well, it was definitely not natural courses, Sir. The Lady in question was apparently a victim of murder. Her body was crushed, and her every bone broken and ground down to powder.'

'But how? Oh, God, no one liked her but to murder her?'

'I believe there had been some sort of argument recently?'

'Argument? That would be a huge understatement, she had us all in uproar. She had threatened to cancel the wedding. Everything was arranged. It was to be a state ceremony and she decided she didn't like the matches.'

'Her daughters and the two gentlemen?'

'Indeed, she felt they deserved titled husbands, after all, I suppose one daughter did marry the Prince. The irony is that those boys were on the Birthday Honour's list. They were to be Knighted. She didn't know that though, it's always kept secret.'

The D. C. I. raised his bushy eyebrows at this revelation. He shook his head and reflected at the sadness of this situation. Someone had died and for nothing.

'Thank you, sir, I hope you realise that there will be some disruption in the palace as we have many people to interview. It would seem she upset a lot of people. Yourself included.'

'Yes, I was very angry. Cinderella thought she would be able to talk her round, but she was nowhere to be found, until now, that is.'

'Seemingly she had many enemies we have to investigate that as well. We will need a formal statement from yourself, the Prince and the out riders that were with you.'

'Of course you must, and the palace is at your disposal. You can set up command here? We have internet and plenty of phone lines if that helps.'

'Thank you, Sir, that is very useful. I will leave you with this officer to take your statement if that is alright?'

The King nodded, and D.C. I. Crumb took his leave. Bloody hell, he thought to himself as he bowed his way out of the Kings presence. Who would have expected a Goblins to have access to the palace of the Fairy King? But then again It isn't often that members of the royal household or their close relatives were murdered. He made his way to the west tower and set about coordinating setting up of the command room. Let's face it Goblins don't have the best of reputations. They have always been considered as the bad boys of Fairy world. Very misunderstood, they were of course very nosy and as such often made great policemen.

Ella and Charley were sitting in their apartments. 'Who would do such a thing?' Ella asked for the hundredth time. 'She was sometimes a right bitch but still she had her good points.'

'She did? I never saw any but, then you knew her better, you were brought up with her.'

'Oh God, I feel really bad now that I thought making her stand up and curtsey so much last time she was here, was so funny, a bit of revenge for the way she treated me as a child. How pathetic is that? She wasn't that bad. It is understandable that she would favour her daughters above me isn't it?'

'My darling, you didn't kill her. She was not liked at all. The Goblins are an excellent police force and they will discover what happened. Don't go trying to find that out, you have your own grieving to do. I am here for you and just want to look after you.'
A sad smile played across her full lips as the tears still fell from her blue eyes, making the Prince just want to take her into his arms and wipe away all the sadness.'

All was quiet in the parlour of Hardwick manor. Esme and Gris were in their room crying large gulping, screeching discordant tears. They loved their mother, just tried to avoid her rages. Their tears were not just for her though, would they still be able to get married?

25

With the wedding so close would it be proper to have a big celebration at such a time? They desperately wanted the wedding to go ahead. The thought of having their own households where they didn't have to put up with their mother's temper was very appealing. Their husbands to be may not have been titled but they were rich and adored the girls.

The Baron was in his parlour nursing a large brandy. He at least had not lost his ability to shut out the noise from the room above. A cultured ability brought about with the help of a spell he had purchased from the Fairy Godmother many years hence. He found it useful when the women in his life were arguing. Or when they laughed. A sound he equated to that of a barn owl when it screeched in the night or a fox's bark. In the hush of this room his sadness reached new depths. She had been a handful, but he knew she loved him in her way and he had loved her in return.

They were good together and apart from her rages jogged along well. She had supported him when money was tight using her own to help with some urgent repairs on the Manor house. He understood why she married him. She was a widowed mother and as such was vulnerable and not just to gossips. She liked the fact that he had a title even if he was an impoverished Baron.

She had engineered their meeting and was charming, good company and very pretty. He knew that she was calculating and had taken time to investigate him and his circumstances. She didn't need money but needed a husband. He had wanted a mother for his only daughter. At first Cinderella had been pleased to have two brand new sisters of much the same age. As time went on the Baron noticed that the only new clothes that came into the house were for Gris and Esme. Ella had their old ones. The girls had beautiful horses to ride but Ella rode an elderly heavy cob. She told him she was happy with that, but he could see her painful hurt.

Every little barb would break her a little bit more and the Baron had watched this happen. But he knew it was no more than Madeline favouring her own daughters above Ella. He tried to treat Ella to more things and spend more time with her to make up for it. She never held a grudge though, she was wonderful to Madeline. He felt guilty now, that he had allowed this to happen to his daughter but had been helpless against Madeline's stronger personality. He was going to miss his wife, her company, her intelligent conversation, and even her temper. Of experience he knew his sadness would fade with time but right now he was incapable of moving from this chair, so deep was his pain.

He had not heard the banging of the huge door knocker, having laid the quiet spell on his room. But the servants had been aware and knew there would be many visitors. Rose opened the door to Richard and Stuart Prentiss. The two beaus of Griselda and Esmerelda. The gentlemen stood on the door step and Rose ushered them into the parlour where the Baron still stared into the unseen wilderness of misery. They stood and waited for him to notice them which he did when the parlour door closed, not too quietly by Rose hoping to break the spell.

'Oh, my boys, how are you?' He asked them. 'Do sit down. Has Rose gone to fetch the girls?'

'Thank you, sir,' they both said in unison Taking a seat on the sofa. 'Please accept our most sincere condolences sir.' Stuart said.

'Thank you. Has Rose…? Oh, I just asked that didn't I? I expect they will be down presently.'

The door burst open and both girls tried to squeeze into the room at the same time. This brought a small smile of reminiscence the face of Brian Hardwick. They always wanted to be first into the room, neither giving way. Nothing changes. He shook his head in sadness.

Esme ran straight into the open arms of Richard and Gris to Stuart. They were still crying loudly and were inconsolable. The young men just held on to his respective lady and waited until the tears subsided.

'Do we have any further information on the status of the wedding Sir?' Richard asked.

'We have to wait until the police have at least started with their enquiries. We will know more then. The King believes it can go ahead. I just hope he is right. I know you all want it.'

'I don't know how I will feel Walking up the aisle and being happy when Mum is dead.' Esme said dramatically flinging her arms wide making Stuart duck to avoid her hand.

'Me neither.' Echoed Gris. 'She was actually going to try to stop it, wasn't she?'

'That was only her anger talking, she didn't really want to put a stop to your wedding. She was a bit drunk as well, and you know what she was like when she had too much to drink.' Baron Hardwick told her.

'I'm sure she would want you to be happy and would really love to see a smile from you as you marry me.' Stuart said.

'It's a lovely day, why don't you all go for a nice walk in the gardens, you don't want to be sitting around with me being miserable.' suggested the Baron.

'Papa, you mustn't be miserable, Mummy would hate that even more. Why don't we all go and see Ella, maybe she has more news.' Esme suggested.

'You go my dears, I will just sit here for a while longer.'

As the two young couples reached the gates Richard spoke up for the first time. 'Your poor Papa is very sad, isn't he?'

'Well we have been a family for a long while, Gris and I have come to love him as our father. I know Mum thought more of him than she would let on.'

'And he thought the world of her, despite her leading him a dog's life most of the time.' Esme said

'Not most of the time, but she often treated him nastily.' Gris replied.

On arrival at the palace they were fortunate that Ella had just been to see the Goblins police and given her statement of the last time she saw her step mother.

She flung her arms around her sisters and they sobbed together, much to the embarrassment of the brothers. They went to her apartments and were seated in her parlour, the atmosphere of sadness prevailed but Ella thought she may as well try to brighten it. By telling them of the Kings plans, once the tea had been served and the servants left the room.

'His majesty has given the go ahead for the wedding, he has been informed by the police that once they have taken statements from everyone they will be out of our hair They can continue their investigations back at their headquarters. So, we can carry on with the arrangements. That's if you feel able to do so. It's only a month away now.'
Esme and Gris brightened visibly, and both said in unison that they wanted to go ahead with it. Richard and Stuart were pleased as well. Ella, in her usual way was pleased she could bring good news to her sisters. After all it wasn't their fault that they were spoiled. The Wicked step mother had done that.

And now they had to live without her spoiling them, but she also knew that the Prentiss brothers would try to continue the good work. They were wealthy enough with their communications business that was the Fairy equivalent of the big Upworld one. Their logo was not of a piece of fruit with a bite taken out of it but of a small Fairy door that was open, and they had called it Infracom. Their strap line was. 'Open communication.' Nearly every Fairy carried one of their phones and children played on the same kind of tablets as the

Upworlder children. Ella often wondered if they had spies in the Upworld factory.   So that they could bring out the latest innovation of computer devices in synchronicity with the other side or did they illicitly use magic? Either way these young men were very wealthy, and she had the satisfaction of knowing that her sisters would want for nothing, the visit was short because the young couples were expected back at the Manor that afternoon to talk to the police.

Chapter 5

The King had felt as if he had the weight of the world on his shoulders. The costs of the wedding were mounting up and not only that, emails were flying backwards and forwards from wedding guests. They had heard of the murder and each was wondering if the wedding was still going ahead. Many had already cancelled saying that they worried about their own personal safety and yet more wanted details of the security that would be put in place.

The Queen was another bother for him. She just didn't seem to be in the real world at all. He knew she was unable to cope with much in the way of unrest. But she was doing her disappearing act more often. Her gin deliveries had increased and the 'Juniper tea' was always evident when he visited her apartments. He for one, was glad the wicked Madeline Hardwick was dead and out of the way at last. She had been a thorn in his side for too many years, but what a horrible way to die, no one deserved that however evil they had been in life. He had always hated her, and since Ella and Charley married, she had been a constant visitor to the palace. He found it very difficult to be polite to her. Her oppressive nature prevailed over the whole palace leaving a deep depression behind her which was exhausting. How did Brian Hardwick manage? He was a cheerful soul but faced with that whenever he went home must have been wearing in extreme.

The King was expecting his Personal Private Secretary any minute, so they could compose an email to answer all the questions from the guests. It was beyond his imagination to compose such a thing alone. It was so much easier when you could send a message by horse drawn carriages or riders. One didn't expect a reply for several weeks. Which would give a poor beleaguered King time to think of replies. But everything was instant now. He often had to make snap decisions. He didn't have so many trusted advisers either. Often, he would turn to Charley and Ella for advice. They seemed to be in touch with technology to a far greater extent. But, in this case, they were dealing with grieving families. Ella was sad, after all this woman had been the closest she had to a mother. Awful as that sounds. He knew she was trying to be strong to support her father and sisters.

His dear old friend Brian Hardwick was grieving for the loss of his wife. He would also face an empty house when the sisters married. They would go and live in the mansions provided by their wealthy husbands. The King felt bad for him. Ella had done well to introduce these two couples and he saw genuine feelings between the young people. He was content that they all were marrying for love. Unlike his own marriage, that had been a union of two factions, which brought at first an uneasy peace but as time went on, full integration between the two Fairy tribes. In that sense his marriage had been a success.

In all other aspects though it was an unmitigated failure. The Queen, for the sake of her race, had sacrificed her love for the man she felt she was destined to marry. The King in turn had tried to make it up to her and had in time found a love and respect for her. But he knew this was not reciprocated. She despised him. Before she took to the gin their relationship was tumultuous. But she took solace in the drink and although he worried about her health, she was much easier to be with. That's the only reason he tolerated her drinking. He shook his head trying to clear his thoughts and started to make yet another list.

Earlier that morning D. C. I. Crumb had hovered by the proffered seat in the Queens apartments. He refused the juniper tea that was offered. Looking around while he waited for the Queen to settle into an easy chair by the fire, he noticed that this room looked very much like a Victorian parlour. A large settee dominated the room but there were small tables with collections of ornaments all dotted about. One couldn't walk straight across the room but had to manoeuvre around obstacles. On one small round table he saw a large stuffed bird in a glass domed casing. On another a collection of scent bottles, and snuff boxes on a further one. Heavy velvet curtains hung halfway across each window cutting out a lot of the daylight. The room was in semi darkness. He found it suffocating and oppressive.

'Your majesty, I wonder if you could tell me a little about the last time you saw Madeline Hardwick?'

'Odious woman can't abide her. She came barging in here demanding that we cancel the wedding. She was very drunk and could hardly stand straight. Didn't even make an effort to curtsey. The woman considers she is so much higher than the rest of us, you would think she was some kind of deity. Oh yes, she is dead, isn't she? Well which ever after life she enters, I hope they are ready for her, that's all.'

'So, she caused some consternation within the palace regarding the wedding?'

'Consternation? How very understated of you Mr. Crumb.'

'Detective Chief Inspector, Ma-am.'

'Oh, yes, so sorry. Detective Chief Inspector.' The smile immediately disarmed him. She really was quite beautiful when she smiled. 'Are you sure you wouldn't like some of my tea?'

'Thank you Ma-am but no. Baroness Hardwick was not here for long then?'

'No, as I said, she crashed her way in, shouted at me and breezed out, rather unsteadily. That was it really. I haven't seen her since and luckily I don't have to see her too often at all.'

'Thank you Ma-am. I shall not disturb you further. I will leave this officer to take a formal statement from yourself and your Personal Private Secretary, if that is alright?'

As he rose and bowed, he noticed she was already looking in to the far distance and had lost concentration. Good luck to Constable Girnt getting that statement, he thought. It may take some time.

'Princess Ella is available to see you now.' Buttons told him as he left the Queen's rooms. 'I can show you the way to her apartments.'

'Good afternoon Detective Chief Inspector. Do sit down.'
What a difference this room was to the Queen's, a light bright room with a couch and two easy chairs set around the fire. A small modern oak coffee table was set in front of the couch. Some nice pictures on the wall and white thin curtains were looped back beside the windows which gave a superb view of the grounds surrounding the palace. A couple of side tables on which were photos of her family.

'Thank you Ma-am.' He replied. 'Please accept my condolences. May I just take you through the last time you saw your Mother?' The cloud of pain that crossed her beautiful face made him regret he had decided to head the investigation himself.

'Well, last time I saw her she was here with my sisters deciding on final materials for the dresses. She stayed in the parlour, instead of coming to the work room. So, I was dashing in and out with various pieces of material for her approval. She seemed quite tired when she left, and I could see she was boiling up.'

'Boiling up?'

'Sorry, it's just what we always used to say when we could see she was about to get into a rage. It was always a time to scatter to all other parts of the Manor house, so we didn't get caught in the cross fire as Esme would say.'

'So, she was becoming agitated then?'

'Yes, I suppose that is a gentle way of putting it. To my shame I had been popping in and out of the room quite a lot. Each time I entered she would have to rise and curtsey. I had enjoyed seeing her in some discomfort. But I feel terrible about that now. It did occur to me that Esme and Gris would take the fall out, so to speak. But when I thought that also my Father would get a back lash, I stopped and had a servant bring all the samples through. Her rages were well known to go on for days. But she didn't often drink either. Father says she was drunk.'

'Your P.P.S. Buttons brought the items in?'

'No, Buttons was not working here then, he arrived later that day to take up his duties as my P.P.S. He was still seeing out his notice at Hardwick Manor.'

'Ah I see. And you didn't see her again?'

'No, I heard she had returned to the palace, but I didn't see her. Esme phoned me to say she was on her way but by the time I got to the Queens apartments she had gone. I never saw her again.'

'Thank you, you have been very helpful. I will need to have that all written down in a formal statement when Constable Girnt has finished with the Queen.'

'He may be a while then. Will you need this room to talk to Buttons?'

'No, thank you, most of the servants are coming to the incident room to give their statements. Thank you for your time and once again, I'm sorry for your loss.' As he left the room, he looked at his list, and realised he had seen all the family now in the palace, as he had talked to Prince Charming prior to visiting the Queen. He could get out of here and make his way to Hardwick Manor. This was going to be the worst one as he heard the Baron was distraught. Knowing what he now did about Madeline Hardwick, he found this amazing. But the chap had been married to her for hundreds of years. D.C.I. Crumb supposed one could get used to anything however bad and miss it when it is torn away.

'Some lunch at the pub, then on to Hardwick Manor constable.' He said to his companion. He hoped the Baron had gathered the family together as he had been asked to.

Chapter 6

Esme, Gris and their beaus arrived back at the Manor in high spirits. Brian Hardwick could hear them giggling and joking as they approached. He smiled to himself. The wedding must still be on then, he thought.
This was confirmed as they all bundled into the parlour.

'Oh Papa, it's all going to be alright. The police said that there was no need to delay and the King has given his permission for the wedding to go ahead.' Esme trilled as she came into the room. The atmosphere had lifted considerably amongst the young people and he was pleased for them. But he resented their joy. He tried to smile with them, but the black cloak of despair would not lift from his shoulders. He pasted on a happy face for their sakes. The girls were very excited, and the Prentiss brothers had picked up on their happiness. They all went off to the kitchen as they had missed their lunch.

Oh, the shallowness of youth, from abject misery to joy with one small decision. The Baron wondered if the girls would miss their mother, she had only just died and all they worried about was getting married, in a big posh do. He looked at the ormallo clock on the mantle and decided he had time for a wander around the gardens before the Detective Chief Inspector was due to arrive. He needed the comfort and peaceful solace his garden gave him. He could easily lose himself there, with plans and dreams of what the summer would bring. Even on a cool spring day. The cheerfulness of the daffodils waving at him would normally brighten his demeaner. Take him away from the bickering of his wife, when she was in one of those moods. The servants would know by watching his actions while viewing the laid-out lawns and neat flower beds, what to expect from their mistress. At precisely two o'clock he returned to his parlour to await the arrival of this policeman.

D. C. I. Crumb expressed his sorrow for the Baron's loss. Before asking any questions.

'When you arrived home on the day you last saw your wife, was she already in the temper that has been described to me?'

'She was not only in one of her rages, but she was also very drunk. My wife was not a big drinker normally and so it would not take much to make her drunk. She was slurring and staggering somewhat. We had words and she crashed out of the house soon after. Apparently, she had been up to the girls and informed them that she was going to cancel the wedding. I heard the front door slam and watched her weave across the lawn towards the Enchanted Woods.'

'Did you follow her?'

'No, I didn't. I thought the fresh air would do her some good.'

'So, let me get this right. You let your very drunk, angry wife walk into the Enchanted Woods alone? Did you not think she may be in danger?'

'If you had known my wife Detective Chief Inspector Crumb, you would know just why I left her to it. I have intervened before and been subject to severe beatings from her. I had thought she would never be attacked when in one of her rages, she was not vulnerable. She would come better off than any attacker, usually with just a look.'

'Except this time.'

'Yes, except this time. But do we know how she died yet?' How she came to be crushed?'

'Not that the pathologist can see so far. She seems to have been subjected to a spell of some kind. '

'But who would use a spell? They are illegal outside the spell school and factories. I didn't know anyone without a degree in it would have the knowledge any longer, and don't you have to be licensed?'

'Indeed. So that was the last time you saw your wife, heading for the Enchanted Woods?'

'She would go that way to reach the palace, which apparently, she was heading for, there is now a well-worn path through to the palace. The girls often go that way to see Ella. Of course, I will be the only one using it in future.'

'But you didn't foresee any danger to your wife?'

'No, Inspector. She was well capable of looking after herself. Any one getting in her way would feel the full force of her vile temper.' Brian Hardwick was beginning

41

to get a little bit annoyed at this line of questioning. Was this man making out that Madeline's death was his fault? He was feeling guilty enough about not following her immediately without the Inspector rubbing salt into the wound.

'The point is Inspector, this had happened innumerable times and she had always come home, so why should I feel that this time would be any different?'

'It was a habit of hers to wander in the Enchanted Woods?'

'When she was in a rage, yes. I could tell by the fact that there was no bird song if she was in there in a temper. Even the animals hid from her. No wolf would care to go near her.'

'There are wolves in the Enchanted Wood?'

'Ha, not now, and I think she may have something to do with that. They migrated to distant shores soon after she moved in with me at Hardwick Manor.'

The Detective Chief Inspector was just beginning to see what sort of person the Wicked step mother could be. He had heard rumours of course as had all of Fairy land. But now he was getting a picture that went against the grain of all he had believed. He, like the King marvelled at the patience and fortitude of the Baron. And thought of his own sweet wife who would not say boo to a goose. His respect for Brian Hardwick grew because he now was seeing the true nature of the deceased.

'How often did the Baroness have these rages? '

'Oh, not so often these days, when Cinderella first married the Prince it was constant. She had mellowed considerably. But often when she went to the palace, I could see she was on the boil.'

'But it didn't always materialize?'

'No, sometimes we could talk her out of it before she bubbled over, so to speak. The girls were quite adept at spotting the signs and usually managed to calm her, before I arrived home.'

'So, when the girls married and moved out you would be left to deal with the aftermath of anything that could cause her to have a rage?'

'Rose, her maid was also very good at easing her out of her temper. I could as well but, didn't on that day and to my bitter regret I argued with her.'

'Well thank you Baron Hardwick. I think I have enough to be going on with. Perhaps I might be able to see your daughters and their intended husbands next?'

'I will have Rose send them down to you, all together? Or one at a time? If you need me any more today, I will be in my garden. Good day D. C. I. Crumb.' The Baron stood and put out his hand to shake the inspector's. Which was a surprise to the Goblins. These Fairy folks were not usually so polite.

He went on to interview the younger fairies and had established to his own satisfaction the time line of the Baroness' movements before she went for that fateful walk. He decided to head back to the command room and have a look at the statements already written up.

Chapter 7

D. C. I. Crumb gathered all the police force that were available to work on this case. He must get a result, and soon. This was by far the biggest case he had dealt with in his long service. He was wondering if it had been a good idea to head the investigation himself. Maybe it would have been better to leave it to his most successful Detective Inspector.
But he felt that as royalty was involved it would look out of place if he didn't take it on. As if it was not important enough, which it most certainly was.
Talking to his assembled crew he said.

   'The good point about this investigation is that we know the back story of most of the people around the Baroness. There only remains the two Prentiss brothers to look into. They are the only unknowns. So, we need someone to dig into their past and see if there is anything we can find out that we need to know.' Two hands went up and those officers were assigned that task. 'Next, we need someone to have a good look at the data base to see if there have been any crimes involving spells. Who is still using spells, and where are they? They are not so easy these days, many of the spell books have been lost over time or destroyed in the reformation years.' Three more hands were raised.

'Good, now, motive. Plenty of the suspects have motive. Not least her daughters and their partners. She had threatened to cancel the wedding. The King and Cinderella as well as the Prince all have motive. They would have been angry and embarrassed at such a move. Maybe even the Queen although I think she is not mentally capable of committing murder. Who wants to investigate more into the motives? You Sergeant Proctor? Very good. The Baron strikes me as being very plausible but that may be a cover. Maybe he just got fed up with the woman and her rages. Which by all accounts were violent and extreme? I need someone to follow him. He is my main suspect at the moment. I just don't believe someone could put up with all that for so many years and not break out. He seems to be grieving but is that guilt as well?'

When a hand went up for that task, the Detective Chief Inspector asked if anyone else had any thoughts.

One constable got up. 'Sir, should we check the phones?'

'Very good, get on to the providers and check that out. All mobiles and landlines to see who had been phoning whom. There may be a link to some magic circles and spell peddlers. The Post Mortem shows bruising and her bones were crushed to the point of not being recognizable. We need to find out how that could happen in a perfectly peaceful clearing in the Enchanted Woods. It must be a spell of some sort. Although I have never heard of a death spell, personally. Anyone know of contacts who may be able to provide information

45

about that? If any of you think of anyone then just get whatever information you can from them. I don't want to know where it came from at this stage. Go to it folks. Let us get this one sown up before this blessed wedding.'

   With that all the constables, sergeants and inspectors got down to their allotted tasks.
More statements were coming in and finally one from the Queen. It read like a novel. The deranged woman could not keep her head in one place for more than two sentences. Poor Constable Girnt was due a day or two off after that marathon.   The Chief read it and put it aside to read again, but there really was nothing useful in there. It was all so much whimsical nonsense. The King's was precise and economical. He told the story and remembered it word for word, nothing changed from the initial interview.

  The Prince's was the same, like father like son. Straight forward no nonsense details of events as he knew them. Cinderella's was a little bit more emotional but still gave the facts. All would have legitimate motives. Get rid of the thorn in the side and get this wedding over with.

   He had asked the two brothers about their feelings about the possible cancellation of their wedding. Both had said they had been angry, puzzled and shocked. They were annoyed that the Baroness would think they were not good enough for her daughters. They were also sad at the thought of not being with their respective brides. Definitive motive for both.

Esmerelda and Griselda both had very powerful motives. They were the ones likely to be most affected by the cancellation. They would not be able to move away from their mother, they would not be able to marry their rich husbands. They may be forced into marriages that were not to their liking. Just to obtain a title. Yes, so many reasons to do away with her.

And the Baron, had he just cracked under the constant pressure of an unpredictable wife? Was this the final straw? Was his grief genuine? It certainly looked as if it was, but the D. C. I. had experienced such grief before in his career and it had proved false. Put him on the yes to motive pile. Along with the trusted servants of all these people. Buttons would want to protect his mistress. He and Dandini were also in the frame to have a motive. Rose the maid, could she have finally decided she had been abused one time too often? So many here that had reason to kill her. But who had access to ancient spells. Truth is any of them could.

Chapter 8

At their monthly strategy meeting Richard and Stuart Prentiss with their company managers and directors were seated around an octagonal table. They were looking at the plans for the launch of their new product. It was a new smart phone which would negate the need for a health monitor. If the phone was linked to the individual all the step, heart rate, oxygen absorption rates, sleep awareness, blood sugar levels, cholesterol and blood pressure apps were already installed. All the new owner needed to do was to hold it to their wrist for a few minutes and the apps would activate. There were alarms for danger points in the health of the owner as well. The advertising was to be based around saving on the time of hard-pressed doctors.

Stuart, in charge of the advertising budget and who also liked to have a hands on approach to the advertising, was directing his team to push the marketing of the new device.

'We have prime time T.V. commercials currently airing and radio interviews also. We secured some Upworld actors of note to promote the phone. 'Kill-imp' which I am reliably informed will be the next block buster movie out has product placement. In fact, we have a scene where the main actor checks his vital signs with it. The ads for cinema which are shown just before the main film will feature that scene.' Sitting back feeling proud of his achievements he looked at the faces around the table. To his right was Richard who as managing Director and chairman of the company had made the decision for the table shape. He was a great reader and liked the stories of King Alfred and the round table. But just to be a little different he opted for the octagonal instead.   Especially designed for the board room and make of the finest Upworld solid oak. Toward the other end of the room were two leather chairs which the brothers used for their private conversations. Between these soft and luscious easy chairs was a small table also octagonal and made of the same oak. Richard glanced across to the chairs and thought he saw one of the cushions shift slightly. Trick of the light he told himself.

'Very good Stuart, I think there will be plenty of coverage there,' he said.
Looking to his right at Dieta Crance, the technical Director. 'Dieta, I hope there are no last-minute glitches and we will be able to launch on time. We are looking at Whitsun weekend which is when the film comes out as well'.

'No hold ups from our end,' Dieta said. 'The Staff have all been issued with one and they have all reported that it works very well. The phone is excellent, the messaging service is great, online it has the latest capability and can be upgraded with any new services for two years. But then we don't want people keeping them for more than two years. Social media is a breeze with it and the health apps are doing a great job. Battery life has been extended to make sure the app doesn't crash.'

Human resources Director Hilary Whentt cut in. 'In fact, we have saved many man hours within the staff as they have been monitoring their health and have not been Taking time off sick. The in-house medical team have reported that more workers are coming in to report problems before they get ill. We have needed more staff in the medical centre but that is still better than the lost working hours. All departments have reported better attendance and less sick days taken. '

 Bruen Walken the Resources and Production Director spoke next. 'We have secured a cheaper supply of the components, same quality though. They have been thoroughly tested by Tech and are up to scratch.'

'Good because it will take a month or two to see a profit on this item, as although we had the original idea from our friend, we did have to do a lot of research and development ourselves.' Richard said.

'Pre-order sales are already above our projected figures and I just hope production can keep up with the future sales.' sales director Fred Drake put in. There was always a bit of rivalry between him and Bruen.
Trevor Matten the Chief security officer spoke next after indicating that he needed the recording and monitoring device turned off. Now nothing would be recorded either in sound or note writing. He indicated that the Accounts Director was to talk next.

'Talking of our friend.' said the person with the most appropriate name for his job. The accounts director Don Money. 'We have always paid into a dedicated bank account, but he has informed me that he has been buying shares in Infracom all this time. He owns quite a decent percentage of the company now. He has also stated that he will be retiring once this item has been launched. This will be the last payment due to him as contracted, upon launch. '

'He has been good for the company and we need to make sure he is happy with the arrangement. I don't want any bad feeling. He deserves to be paid handsomely for the work he has done especially as he will not get ongoing royalties.' Richard said.

'It's a shame he is thinking of stopping but I suppose the time is right.'

'I do wonder at his anonymity and just why he wishes for that. You would have thought an inventor of his calibre would have wanted the fame that went with the fortune. He has given us four really good products and we have been able to bring them out well in advance of anything the Upworld company has that matches.' Stuart mused.

'Yes, I don't know his real identity, but he has brought us some great stuff.' Don said.

'So, launch, is Whit Weekend when my brother and I will be back from our honeymoons. Now gentlemen the next thing on the agenda is Stuart and me Taking early retirement. We have already discussed this, and you have all been issued with five percent of the company's value in shares. If you wish to make a director's buy out or retire yourselves and sell your shares when we put ours up for sale, it is up to you. The offer from the Upworld company is also worth considering. This has all been said before, I am just reiterating the agreement.

As you have seen in the future it won't be so easy to come up with new products before the Upworld company does. We will not have the insight. The new phone will be profitable for a good few years. Please take independent advice. But as soon as the shares hit the highest point, we think that will be after the launch which will be just before the Upworld company launches their own product, we will be selling. This company has made us and our friend very rich. Good luck everyone.'

'He has always been loyal but has mentioned that he was offered more money from a rival.' Don said.

'Has he ever told you exactly where and how he gets his ideas?' Stuart asked.

'No, he won't say but I don't think he is using old fashioned magic. Maybe mind reading or some kind of transference? He has certainly produced the goods and has not failed us.   As previously we will be able to launch the new phone before the Upworlders do. He has the ability to become invisible I know that much, and I think he also is trying out shape shifting, but I'm not sure how far he has got with that.' Don told them.

'Good grief, he is very talented but who is teaching him all this stuff? It has been outlawed for hundreds of years and very few are licensed to use magic now.'

Richard and Stuart were amazed at the revelations. Richard glanced again at the easy chair and was sure he saw movement.

'Right then gentlemen, lunch time. Stuart and I have other things to discuss so we will meet you in the restaurant in half an hour,' Richard stated.

Everyone got up from their chairs and left the room, Don being the last out found difficulty shutting the door first time. It was as if something was in the way. But eventually he managed to close it. The being that had blocked it was safely out. He had heard what he wanted to hear and would double his shareholding. He now had to get outside the building and remove the shield of invisibility. Not an actual cloak you understand but a spell that meant no one could see him.

Richard and Stuart stayed in the board room, keeping the recording devises turned off, they had other things to discuss.

'Do you think the time is right?

'Yes, it is getting more difficult, so now would be a good time. The share price will rocket with the launch of the new product. Time to sell and get out. Early retirement, marriage and a new phase in life for us both.'

Lord Middlemass walked into his gentleman's club and ordered a large whiskey. His future was now secure. He could happily retire. He feared he was about to be exposed in Upworld as well. He had been working in the Upworld research and development department. He wondered what the Brothers would do if they realised that he was not an inventor. That he had stolen the plans and documents for their last four products from the biggest of the Upworld communication companies. This new one being the fourth he had 'invented', but the time was right to get out, and before he was revealed as the spy the Upworld had been searching for. He wanted to continue his studies in ancient magic. He was still not able to become invisible at will. As for shape shifting, he had only just started working on that. And, most of all, he wanted to go home. Living in the Infraworld was all very well but his home is in Upworld. He was an interloper in this world. But he needed to be here to learn magic.

The Fairy Godmother was his only contact with the ancient spells although she would not divulge them to him. But that book he found, that ancient spell book. Little did she know it, but her teachings were enabling him to interpret the writings. She knew all the spells and was making a very good living by teaching interested parties in the ancient arts. She was proficient at making new spells. Which she sold on, but nothing powerful. Just your everyday stuff. He knew that behind that little shop front in the centre of town there was an enormous factory, where she employed Imps to make the spells. Each room only made one part of the spell and she always did the finishing touches. That way no one could just copy them and if they tried, they would just fail as they didn't have all of it.

She sold potions, in her shop under license. Normal innocuous stuff for the innocent and enchanted. Love potions. Health giving compounds, beauty potions that were said to rid the face of wrinkles. But Lord Middlemass knew about the workings behind the shop which was set in a small tree lined street. Each of the buildings contained a small shop, there the haberdashery, then the butcher and going on to the green grocer. Each one with its own door onto the street, and small as you would expect, with their wares spilling onto the path.

All except Spellbinding. Her shop. When inside there were massive rooms, filled with shelves. For bottles, jars and packets of spells, cleaning products and medicines. Up the internal stairs was a huge mansion where she lived with her workers. She was loved and looked after them well. They were loyal and kept her confidence. Not many people knew about the workings inside the shop, they only saw the small windows set behind the branches of the trees and bushes. There was a country residence as well. Somewhere in the Enchanted Woods. He knew where that was because he had partaken in lessons there and often saw the Queen there.

Now that the Wicked step mother had been disposed of and the wedding was to go ahead, he could relax. Those boys had only decided to retire from the business and sell up because they were to be married. Their new life beckoning. If they had stayed single they would have wanted to carry on and probably expand their business, he would have been trapped into the old life, the double life. Without her interfering he was free to give it all up, and follow the ancient black arts.

Chapter 9.

Dan and Buttons were cuddled up together on the couch in Dan's apartment. They had eaten a fine meal, leftovers from the dinner that Ella and Charley had also enjoyed. The cook always made far too much and today it was Dan's turn to take the first pick. Some very acceptable wine came with it and both were replete. Their apartments were not only in the same block but next door to each other. And as high-ranking servants they were allocated decent accommodation.

Each apartment had a big lounge and dining area with a kitchenette, a big bedroom with an en-suite bathroom. Furnished with old but extremely good quality furniture. Whenever the palace had under gone any restoration or upgrading the old furniture was moved to the servant's quarters.

'So, had the Queen always been this way?' Buttons asked.

'Ever since I've known her, yes. She wanders about the palace in a daze most of the time and you can bow, say good morning, as much as you like but she never notices you. Just wanders past. She doesn't seem to be able to walk in a straight line but sort of bounces off the walls as she goes. She is very drunk nearly all the time. I really don't know how she manages to carry out all her royal duties. She always seems to be able to shake it off for visits and functions but whenever she is in her rooms, she is blotto'

'How does the King deal with that?'

'I think he has just got to the point of no longer caring. So long as she doesn't embarrass him outside the palace. How about the Baroness, was she always such a bitch?'

'It was worse when Cinders first got married, but lately she could be quite pleasant. The Baron and her always got on well enough. She would crack a joke, some dirty ones, if she was in the right mood. Could be very amusing but was just so angry that the story went Cinders' way. She considered it so unjust that it was never mentioned in the story how much she had given to the marriage, both financially and emotionally. As far as the story went, she was a prize bitch from the word go. But I can't see the Baron ever marrying her if he thought she would be cruel to Cinders.'

'You still call her Cinders? How sweet is that.'

'Yeah, I know she adopted Ella, I think it was a way of distancing herself from the story. But she will always be Cinders to me.' Buttons said with a smile.

'Cinders dressed in rags.'

'That's what the story will have you believe. Esme and Gris had designer clothes and Cinders just didn't want them. She was happiest when out in the stable yard and with the animals. She didn't want to be dressed in posh frocks. But as she got a bit older and the girls either grew out of their clothes or got fed up with them Cinders would take them to her work room. She unpicked them all and cut them down to fit her. Not that the girls were fat by any means, but they were always a couple of sizes larger than Cinders. Statuesque you could call them, especially with those honking great feet. '

'Well, can't say I noticed the size of their feet until we went around there with the glass shoe. But of course, the Fairy Godmother had made the shoes to fit Cinderella, so those girls were never going to get in to that one.'

'That was the first time I saw the Wicked step mother in a real temper. If you and the Prince had not whisked Cinders away with you, I really think we would have been dealing with murder then.'

'Oh, blimey. Shit really hit the fan then?'

'You could say that. The Manor house was in turmoil for weeks.'

'So, have you any ideas as to who may have done it?'

'None whatever. No one liked her, and she angered a lot of people trying to cancel the wedding but to go as far as murder?'

'Does seem a bit extreme doesn't it?'

'Just a bit. Any more of that wine there?'

Buttons and Dandini knew their respective families inside out because as we all know they grew up with them. Dan and Charley were brought up together as youngsters. Dan to be a companion for Charley. They were schooled together and as such whenever Prince Charming had a problem, he would talk it over with Dandini. But this problem was something no one could solve with discussion. That didn't stop the gossips in the palace though who all had theories about who had killed the Wicked step mother.

'Rumour has it that the magic used to kill her was from Goblins past. That's the latest story going around the palace anyway.' Dan said.

'Yeah, I heard that one and that the King flew out of the palace and stomped on her.'

'Well at least that has taken over from the lightning bolt theory. Although how they could have come up with that one when there was clean unburned grass all around her, I don't know.'

'Oh, so silly, but what a horrible way to die. There are poisons that can kill instantly, why would someone take pleasure in squeezing the life out of a person?'

'And how? I mean she was in the middle of a large clearing, there are no animals in the Enchanted Woods big enough to harm her, no trees had been felled, nothing around her to do such damage, not even a set of foot prints.'

'Will we ever know?'

'Who can tell?'

Chapter 10

The Queen, having escaped the confines of the palace
again, was in discussion with the Fairy Godmother.
They were Taking tea, real tea, in the large house
behind the Fairy door in the Enchanted Woods. Plans
were being drawn up for Sophia, to leave at last and to
be reunited with Raphael. No-one had remembered
that the Queen had a name, she was always the Queen.
Well, the King, also had a name, but she had forgotten it
with the passing of time. He had been so disparagingly
down beat about the wedding of their only son to
Cinderella, not giving then a grand state wedding.

Sophia was bitterly disappointed, as she knew
Charles had been. Cinderella had just been happy to
marry her Prince. The plan was Sophia her to escape
after their wedding. But as it had not been a state
occasion, no other Infraworld species had been invited.
No Goblins, Imps, foreign Fairies, other story characters.
No-one. They were, however, all coming to this one.
She was thrilled to see that all the characters of Red
Riding Hood were included on the invitation list. Even
the wood man, who killed the wolf. Each time she left
this house she had to put on her old face again. To look
the part. But, she in fact, looked just as she had when
she was torn from the arms of her one true love.

Raphael. She wondered if he had kept his looks, but it didn't matter either way.

'We must get the timing perfectly right for you to disappear.' The Fairy Godmother told her. 'It will have to be during the banquet. After the speeches, the present giving and the cake cutting.'

'But before the happy couples leave for their respective honeymoons. I believe they may be travelling to their Islands in Upworld. Very bold of them.'

'Oh, it's not so dangerous now. There had been communication going on between the two worlds for some time. In fact, didn't you tell me that Cinderella had been invited to participate in London Fashion week in September?'

'Yes, her designs are being adopted by the Upworlders. She seems to have a knack for making clothes that all peoples like.' She will be busy once this wedding is over getting things ready for that.'

'You will not be here to see it though. You will be in another story. Untouchable.'

'How can I be sure to be untouchable? I have already made the transference once to come to this land. Will the Goblins not be able to extradite me from there?'

'That journey was thought of as willing. Although in fact, you had no choice but to come here. As far as the laws are concerned you decided to come of your own free will, even though you were ordered here.'

'So, if I don't want to come back, they can't make me?'

'Not as the law stands, no.'

'At long last I can be the Fairy I was always meant to be. Not a reluctant Queen, but the simple wife of a wood man.'

'It will be a very different life. He is not the richest of men. His woodland cottage is small and a bit dilapidated. But you will still have some magic powers to transform it, if we don't have to wait too long.'

'I hope to never have to use magic again, I have been using it for so long and you have taught me well, but I could do with living the simple life. No longer living a lie.'

'I already have another pupil, so my skills will not be wasted.'

'Oh? Do tell.'

'All I will say is that he has been instrumental in making the two grooms very rich and it has involved Upworld.'

'How can I thank you? I have waited so long for this chance and would not have been able to get this far without you. Without my drops I would have died of alcoholic poisoning by now. With the drops neutralizing the alcohol I could drink the stuff and wander about un-noticed. Unseen as such. Just because I seemed drunk, they would carry on with conversation around me as If I was not there.'

'Well, for a start there is no need for thanks. You have paid me handsomely over the years and I would never have been able to build and equip the shop and factory without that money. I am now self-sufficient which was essential after the Magic Banning laws were brought in. How was a Fairy Godmother ever supposed to make a living without magic, I ask you? And I am sorry that you had to drink all that gin. I could have made a non-alcoholic one for you to drink, but then if someone else decided to partake they would have realised it contained no alcohol. Your cover would have been well and truly blown. We couldn't have that, now could we?'

'I got used to the taste and I don't really dislike it now. Same as I have got used to the King and don't really dislike him either. But I do still hate the restrictive life of a Queen. Soon be back in my lovely woods with my gorgeous wood man.' The Queen mused whimsically.

'He is a bit of a looker with more than a hint of Brad Pitt to him.' The Fairy Godmother raised her eyebrows, looked at the Queen from the side of her eyes and then she smiled.

'Oh, stop it, or I will need to go before the wedding and that would spoil everything,' Sophia said laughing.

'More tea and how about one of my nice coconut cakes?' The Fairy Godmother asked her.

'Hmm that would be lovely. Then I had better make my way back before they send out search parties .It's such a shame that I can't travel back a bit further in time than just a few hours.'

'No, we never did succeed in that one for you, did we? But you have other powers. I'm so glad that disgusting woman's death has not put the wedding off. After all this planning.'

The Queen nodded her agreement as she sipped her tea, staring at the fire in the grate.'

Chapter 11

D. C. I. Crumb was in the office of the chief forensic officer. He was an Elf called Faraday. A very experienced man in his field. He had just about seen everything, but this?

'Every bone?' Crumb asked.

'Every single one, all so much powder. She had been totally crushed, Poor woman it must have been an excruciating death and she would have still been alive to feel the first of the pain. What a way to go.'

'But there was nothing in the clearing that could have crushed her, do you think she was killed elsewhere and dumped there?'

'Not really, as we lifted her, she nearly fell to bits, it was only her clothing that was holding her together. I don't see how someone could have got there in one piece. There were no track marks of vehicles, so she would have to be carried by a person. And there were not even any discernible fresh foot prints in the clearing. No-one had passed through that way until the King and his outriders came upon the scene.'

'Well, thank all the deities he was intelligent enough to call us in before they trampled all over the crime scene. I have never seen anything like this. It looks as if the very trees moved to crush her and moved back again.'

'That's exactly what it does look like, but trees can't just walk.'

'Not unless there is magic being used. Illegal magic. But then again if someone is going to murder a person, the fact that magic is no longer legal won't bother them, it is the least of their crimes. So, the rumours are correct, it must have been magic. What we are looking into is who has a license to teach and practice. There is only the Fairy Godmother, that we can find, in this area. I am going to see her this afternoon in her shop. I hope she can spread some light on this for us.'

'Meanwhile I will get back to the body and see if there is anything else, I can determine.'

Faraday went into the dissecting room where the assistants had pushed two tables together to accommodate the flat pancake like structure that had once been the Wicked step mother. He looked at her and thought he may as well have another look inside, but it was unlikely he would find anything recognizable as an organ in there. The body was black with bruising and he had inflicted many cuts on her with the first examination. It had been almost impossible to see where one could cut to find a particular organ. She looked like a spatchcocked chicken. He would have to fold her over to fit into a coffin. Or they could just lay her over an open fire like a blanket. Not something that immortals needed to worry about normally. He would have to contact Upworld funeral directors to ascertain how to proceed.

D. C. I. Crumb entered the shop of the Fairy Godmother on Tremble street. It was a small one roomed space, but he knew she had more to it. The lady herself rose from a small chair behind her counter and greeted him.

'Detective Chief Inspector, welcome to my shop. How can I help? Terrible thing to happen. We don't see many murders around here, do we?'

'No Ma-am.' he said looking around the tiny shop. He saw one wall dedicated to love potions, all different scenarios catered for. There were emollients and salves for cuts and wounds, beauty products for men and women, embrocation's for aching joints and spurious pains. Scented handkerchiefs, candles, bathing oils, body lotions. Spells for getting the house cleaned, doing the ironing, making sure that a taxi came when required. Every niggling annoyance had a spell to put it right.

Dire warnings came with each spell, reminding the purchaser that there may be consequences for themselves and other people if used too often.   He marvelled at the amount of stock in such a small establishment. But having got inside he realised it was much bigger than it looked from outside. He spotted a rack of wands, and some rodent trespass powder. Nothing to kill he noticed but just to put them off coming into the house. Cold remedies and flu medicine.

In fact, she had everything in here. As he looked around some other customers entered.

He wondered if he would be able to get to talk to her alone, but she called through to a back room for a young Fairy to come and take over serving the customers and beckoned him to follow her behind the counter. The room he entered was a spacious high-ceilinged square lounge area. There were three settees set in a U shape around a large T.V. hanging on the wall.

There was a dining table and some cupboards. Not the sort of room that one would entertain Royalty but a comfortable place to relax in at the end of a busy day. A tray of tea and biscuits was already placed on the table set between the settees. The Fairy Godmother indicated to the D. C. I. to sit down and poured him some tea. Earl Grey, just how he liked it, and ginger nut biscuits, his favourite.
He settled himself on the soft settee and thought he may have difficulty getting up from here, it was so cosy. He had never been further than the shop before and the size of the room took him by surprise.

'Inspector, how is Philomena? I hope the embrocation has taken the pain from her poor knees.'

'It worked well, she is skipping about like a spring lamb. Thank you for asking. The doctors had given up on her knees'

'Oh, good, I thought It must have, as she had not been back. The poor dear was in such pain.' Crumb's wife had purchased many potions and lotions from the shop, in fact although he didn't know it, he was the victim? Is that the right word, no, subject, to a love potion that Philomena bought from here many years ago. She had got very fed up waiting for him to propose and decided to move him on a fraction. But the Fairy Godmother was not about to tell him that. She had a strict confidentiality policy. That way her customers knew that they could trust her never to divulge secrets. She knew of practitioners who had let the cat out of the bag and had got in all sorts of trouble because of it.

'You may be able to help us with a conundrum regarding the death of the Wicked step mother. I know I don't have to tell you that this is all in strictest confidence.'

'Of course not, Inspector, I would be struck off the magic license list of I was to divulge any of this. I adhere to the strictest policy and nothing said inside this, I may say, sound proof room is ever mentioned outside of it. You may speak freely and the oath I took will protect me from telling.'

'Protect you?'

'Yes, indeed, I have need of protection, I have been told so many things in this room that I could be subject to unmitigated horror if it was thought I would repeat any of it, but this room protects me and my clients. You see, it has the power to remove memory. If I was to tell you something that I regretted telling I could ask the room to make you forget it. It also refuses to let memories out if asked prior to the telling. But If I ask the room to divulge them everything will be remembered by both parties. That is why I was able to talk so freely with you just now about your lovely wife. Only in this room.'

'Very useful, I wish we had such a room or even an honesty room down at the station. That would save so much trouble.'

'Shall I look into it for you Inspector?'

'Only joking Ma-am, I think we had better stick to the tried and tested method.'

Taking a deep breath, he carried on. 'The Lady had been squashed, flattened. She had not got a single bone intact they have all been reduced to powder. Do you know of any spells that could do that?'

'Where was she found? I think I heard she was in a clearing in the Enchanted Woods?'

'She was, a very wide clearing. There was nothing found nearby that could have done that to her and the trees are spaced with wide paths between them. The clearing was a perfect circle, most unusual. The grass had not been disturbed and there were no foot prints to be seen.'

'Flat you say? Hmm I have heard of a spell, a very ancient one. It allows the trees to walk. I wonder if they had been instructed to come together?'

'Would we not see evidence of their movement?'

'Oh no, the spell would repair it all. That would seem to be, at least one way of doing such a thing. Either that or a heavy cloud. They can come down and crush people. Or there is even folding earth. There are many ways of crushing a person. But usually they leave some sort of telltale sign. The Heavy cloud for instance would have taken some branches and twigs down with it, they are normally too big for the space when coming down, things get broken. Folding earth often will take more than one, they are mistaken for earthquakes. But my bet is on the Walking trees. There are not many people who have the knowledge, experience and power to conjure up Walking trees, and none that live locally. Other Fairy Lands have some such as me, but we are all very ethical.'

'You teach magic, do you not?'

'Indeed, I do, but I have never touched the ancient spells in my school. I just teach healing and simple conjuring here. It is all my license allows.'

'Thank you, Ma-am, now will I remember this conversation?'

'Divulge.' Stated the Fairy Godmother. 'Now you will Detective Chief Inspector.'

He did notice that she had used his full title this time instead of demoting him to Inspector. He wondered why it was that he hadn't corrected her each time. When he left the Fairy Godmother wondered who could have conjured up such a spell. It was unthinkable that anyone she had taught would know that much magic.

The only person who would find such a thing useful was the Queen, but she didn't have enough power to do that did she? She had been giving Sophia lessons for hundreds of years, but they would never involve killing people. And the sheer power it would take to cast the Walking trees spell, if anyone was around here that

could do that, she, the Fairy Godmother would know.
Wouldn't she?

Chapter 12

Esme and Richard were sitting in the summer house. Richard had just given her a present. One of the new phones. He had put her sim card in it and sent her a love message that she would receive as soon as she turned the phone on.

'Oh, how super is that?' she trilled. 'Is it the same to reply as the old one?'

'Yes, exactly the same. Just hit reply and type.'

'Oh Richard, I can't wait to be married to you. Only a couple of weeks now. You really need to tell me where we are going for our honeymoon. I need to know what to pack.'

'You won't get the secret out of me like that my love. I have already told you that you will only need an overnight case. A very small one. You will have clothes ready for you waiting at our destination. So just a change of undies is all you will need.'

'Oh, how intriguing. You are such a naughty boy. Not telling me.'
She turned her head and looked at him coquettishly and said 'I'm not so sure I want to be married to a man who can keep secrets from me. How will I know that he is being honest with me in the future?'

'Nope, still no good. I'm not telling you.'

The next face she tried was one of a little girl, who can't have her own way. Bottom lip stuck out and staring at him from under her fringe. With a shrug she turned away from him.

Richard laughed. 'No. still not telling.'

With a sigh she gave up for now and decided that she would find out soon enough. She was a bit annoyed because having used all her wiles she had not been able to break him down. That, in itself, was unusual for Esme, she normally got her way especially with the men in her life. But then again she only really had the Baron to practice on and he was a push over. I have a lot to learn, I can see that, she thought. But she did love her new phone. It was even in her favourite colour. Rose Gold. Real gold. She could see the Fairy hall marks. It would be a shame to put in in a case, so you couldn't see the gold.

She mentioned this, but Richard said. 'No need, it is Pixie hardened gold so won't scratch or dent and the glass is hardened and laminated to withstand huge pressure. It is even water proof.

'Are all the ones on the market like that? They will be very expensive.'

'No there are only four like that, yours, mine, Stuarts and the one he has given Gris.'

Laughing Esme said. 'I bet hers is Platinum then.'

'Think so, yes.'

'So, you give me a phone but won't tell me where we are going?'

'No. I. Won't.' He said laughing.

'Oh well it was worth another try. Now give me a kiss.'

Richard took her pretty face in his hands and planted a great big kiss right on her lips. He thought she was pretty, even if she was not a classic beauty like her sister Ella. Her eyes were big, maybe too big for her face and her nose was a little bent from falling off her horse. The one her Mother had bought for her when she was too small to be able to handle it properly. The stunning Arab gelding in the stable. Esme was perfectly able to ride it now that the horse was so much older and more mellow. But her mother had bought it for the look of it and it's true he was a stunning piece of horse flesh. But he had not really been a child's pony. The Mare that Gris owned was also a lovely creature but not a family pony either. Still these horses had taught the girls to ride and they had courage on horseback which both Richard and Stuart admired.

Richard stared at Esme's full lips, they were indeed very kissable and all in all she was put together quite nicely. The not so ugly sisters, he thought. They were of a larger build than Ella, that was true but by no means fat. They both had what he would describe as chestnut hair. And they were both very athletic and had good muscle tone. In fact, in running races they could beat the brothers any time. But then since school days the brothers had spent time building their empire of communication so keeping fit had not been a priority. And these girls had spent most of their life running away from their mother's temper, he thought with a chuckle.

Gris and Stuart were running towards them across the lawn. Gris waiving her phone in the air.

Esme stood and called. 'Platinum?'

'Of course,' panted Gris as they arrived at the summer house. Stuart a few steps behind.

'You realise I let you win then?' he said.

'Phaw, liar,' laughed Gris. Stuart was the younger of the two as was Gris. They had been introduced that way by Ella and it had stuck. Both parties were immediately attracted and so began a long courtship.

'Right, now we are all together,' Stuart said. 'We have something we want to tell you.'

Esme and Gris cast a glance at each other and smiled. Where they about to reveal where they were going for the honeymoon at last?'

The girls took a seat beside each other and putting their hands in their laps in a polite way as they had been taught, they looked at the two brothers expectantly. Stuart started the explanation.

'When we launch these phones to the public, after our honeymoon, we expect the share price to double at least. We have decided that would be the best time to sell our shares in the company. Hand it over and take early retirement.   That does not mean we won't have any money, don't worry, he quickly added, as the look of surprise crossed each girls face. 'We will in fact have more. And we won't have to go to work all the time when we are married. We, my pretties are loaded. Loads a money.'

'Are you keeping some of the shares?' Esme asked. Showing a full understanding of the workings of a business and ownership.

'A few, yes but we have also bought shares in the Upworld company. The one that we have been in competition with'

'We are so excited about all this and we couldn't be happier.' Richard said.

'You will be able to be home with us and not leave us lonely in a huge mansion then?' Gris enquired in a little girl voice. Pretending she was clueless.

'We can travel and enjoy our lives together.' You girls are marrying the richest men in the Infraworld. Your lives will be full of frivolity and comfort.'
Gris, said. 'So, what have you done with the rest of your money that will earn you this massive income?'

'Land, we have bought land. Some rough stuff that we can build houses on. And some working farms that will give us income from the tenancies. Don't you...'

'Don't you dare say, don't worry your pretty little head!' The girls interrupted in unison. Which made them all fall about laughing.   Life was going to be so good from now on. Thank goodness their mother wasn't here to spoil it.

Baron Hardwick heard them all laughing and was cheered that they could be so happy. He just wished it didn't have to be at the expense of his own happiness. He perused his gardens and was checking that the beds were all in order. He loved his garden, his solace when Madeline had been in a mood.

The formal kitchen garden with the raised vegetable beds and soft fruit sections was a great place to wander, tasting the ripening fruits. He was especially pleased with the sweeping lawn leading down to the lake. In the winter the girls would skate on there and in the summer, there were punts to take onto the water. Many picnics had been enjoyed beside the gently lapping shore. But most of all he adored the wild flower garden. Each year it was a profusion of colour that attracted many bees. The picket fence which separated it from the neater and tidier garden showed the beauty of the natural flowers. Madeline had joked that he could grow weeds anywhere. At least he thought it was a joke.

They all went indoors to have a high tea. There the youngsters told the Baron of their plans. He congratulated the boys and asked what the reason was for getting out. He wasn't quite sure he believed them when they told him that their interest had paled, and they were looking for new challenges. There was something else here he thought but he kept that to himself. Like Ella he had been suspicious of how they had brought out new technology just days before the Upworld company did. But so long as they didn't jeopardize the happiness of the girls he wasn't too bothered. He was not particularly looking forward to the wedding. That meant they would all go. He would be alone here in this massive Manor. He had servants of course but they were a bit afraid of the gap between their status. Buttons had been the only one who took no notice of the difference in their standing. But of course, he had followed his heart, to stay in the service of Ella his special friend, and to be partners with Dan. Best of both worlds for Buttons. 'Glad for him,' the Baron muttered to himself. But what would life be like for him, certainly more relaxed that he had thought it would be. With the absence of his wife, but not filled with company, gossip and laughter. He tried to smile and show happiness for the young people but deep inside he ached.

Chapter 13

The investigation was still on going. The poor constables that had been given the task of checking the phone records were going a little bit crazy. Checking and cross checking each person's calls, texts and all social media conversations. That is everybody. Within the Palace and the Manor and extraneous contacts. Some of these messages made extra work as they were to the Upworld, and so permission was necessary to investigate them. D. C. I. Crumb didn't see much of his wife and for that matter his home. There had never been an investigation like it in his experience, but there had never been a crime like this either. He opened the door to his office looking haggard and tired. There stood Philomena with a change of clothes and a pot of her marvellous stew.

'Oh, my dear, what a sight for my poor sore eyes. Will the stew remain hot while I pop down to the changing rooms and take a quick shower?'

'Yes, Solomon, but don't be too long. I will sit here and wait. So, don't go getting distracted and leave me sitting all day.'

Kissing her quickly on her cheek he took the clean clothing and made his way to the basement. Ten minutes to myself, he thought. Stripping off his filthy garments and stepping into a hot shower. Solomon, she called me Solomon, not Solly. Maybe she is just telling me that I have been at work too long. He mused as he washed himself. She had even brought his shaving kit, so once out of the shower he needed to face the mirror.' Oh dear, you do look dreadful,' he said to his reflection. Half expecting it to answer him back, so deep was his exhaustion.

Philomena had laid out a table cloth bowl and spoon for him at his desk and he settled himself down to enjoy her lovely stew.

'Oh, that's so much better. Given me renewed energy. Thank you, my darling.'

'When will you be able to get home? The children have forgotten what you look like.'

'I wish I could say, but give them a kiss from me,' he answered as there was a knock on his door and a young constable popped her head around.

'Sir, I think you need to see this.'
With a sigh Philomena gathered up the empty bowl, spoon, table cloth and his discarded dirty clothes. Gave him a brief kiss and left.

'What have we got then Constable?' he asked, business as usual. Would this be the breakthrough they were all hoping for? Or another red herring?

'Sir, we have been looking into Infracom. Their shares had been subject to consistent aggressive purchases. One individual has been building a good percentage of the stock for the last six months.' The constable told him. 'We don't know if it is relevant but thought you should know.'

'Good, carry on and see if you can detect who it is. Well done. It may not have any relevance but could be useful.'

Privately the D.C.I. thought that it was probably just a canny investor. He himself had purchased shares in the company and was planning on selling them soon anyway. A good boost to his pension. But this is police work and you never know if it has any connection. His thoughts turned to his family. Philomena was right, he will go home tonight. Have a nice evening relaxing in comfort.

Ella and Charles had the same thought. Their days had been so hectic, and they kept missing each other. So, they allocated this evening to themselves.

'You mustn't try to take on all the King's duties, Charley, he needs to be kept occupied. He keeps trying to interfere with the wedding preps. All that he is responsible for has been sorted out already, but he enquired about the bride's transport today. I already have that sorted, courtesy of the Fairy Godmother.'

'I know he is nit picking but he is just doing it to keep his mind off the investigation. There doesn't seem to be much progress there.'

'Well not that we know of, but they have all the resources of the police force handling it. Did you hear about Richard and Stuart selling up when the new phone has been launched?'

'Yes, Mother told me, in one of her few lucid moments. She isn't having many of those lately either.'

'Oh dear, she is dipping into the juniper tea somewhat isn't she?'

'And going on more walkabouts. Anyway, she only managed to tell me so much but what have you heard about The Lads?'

'Well they are sure the share price will double with the launch of the new phone, they always have with every other launch apparently, so are quite confident it will again. Perhaps we should increase our holding before the launch?'

'Oh blimey, you are the money person, if you think we should then do it.' Charley laughed. He always asked if they could afford something if he wanted to buy it, he hadn't got a clue how much was in the bank accounts. It only needed one person to look after the finances and he preferred to leave it to Ella.

'So, when the share prices do this doubling act the boys will sell, on the market? Or do they have a buyer in mind?'

'I don't know but something makes me think it has to do with the Upworld company. Without Infracom they would have a competitor free market. They are by far the biggest in Upworld and would then have the majority of the market share. So maybe the boys are selling out to them?'

'Makes sense I suppose. I know one of the directors and he doesn't seem to think that is the preferred option. But Trevor is going to retire and buy shares in Upworld. The Brother's company has made quite a few people very wealthy.'

'They have done well, but I really do wonder how they always manage to bring out their latest things just before Upworld. I'm sure they must have had a spy in there.'

'Industrial Espionage? Oh Ella, you think so?'

'Yes, I do. Or magic. But their success has been phenomenal, meteoritic. How else would you explain it? Good business heads can only take one so far. I have only just cracked Upworld with the fashions house. And fashion is just as sought after as newest communications.'

'True, how are the preparations going for London?'

'Slowly, but on time, I think. Just need to get this wedding out of the way and see them all away on their honeymoons and I can concentrate on it. I have the designs in sketch form but need to be getting some made up. My best machinists are doing wedding dresses, bridesmaid dresses and suits. But I will be able to move on a pace after wards.'

'What transport have you arranged to bring the brides to the cathedral?' Charley asked.

'The Fairy Godmother is going to replicate my ball pumpkin coach for them. It's all arranged, and the girls are over the moon with the idea. So is Dad. He thought it was a great laugh. I'm worried about him though. He will be alone in the Manor.'

'Should we offer him an apartment in the palace? Just for his work days?'

'We could offer but he loves his garden and I don't think he will leave it. He also likes the walk to the palace, says it keeps him fit.'

'Well, I will try and cut back on what I am Taking off Dad, He does seem better when he is too busy to think too much. He has the guest list finalised again now. There were quite a few cancellations at first, but they have all emailed to say they will be attending. So back to the full compliment. All their accommodation and all those not bringing servants have been allocated newly trained personnel. Some are bringing their own accommodation and space has been cleared in the Enchanted Wood for their mobile homes.'

'Well, sounds like he is on top of all that then. I saw the woodmen clearing some enormous areas for the mobiles. They are not just caravans, are they? Some are bringing bloody great houses. All the services laid on ready for them to connect?'

'Yes, the Fairy Godmother has helped with work spells to make it all easier. All the guests need to do is settle their homes and they will be automatically connected.'

'In that case it looks like we are good to go.'

'When you go to London, shall we have a holiday?' We could take the kids to London, they would love that.'

'Will I organize that? or will you?' Laughing Charley said. 'Oh, I think I can manage that one, so long as expense is no object and I can make it luxurious as well as fun.'

'Spend what you like, we can afford it and I think we deserve it. Roll on September then.' She replied smiling at the thought of a proper holiday.

'Now, don't go wishing your life away Cinderella.' This was an ongoing joke between immortals but as has been proved with Madeline's death. Immortality can be brought to an end.

Chapter 14

D. C. I. Crumb parked outside his house beside the small well cared for front garden. The door of his transport opened for him as did the gate. It knew when he was home. He paused to admire Philomena's hard work with a fine lawn and spring flowers popping up all around the front garden. He and his family lived in a modest semi detached Fairy house, the two doors next to each other in the huge trunk of an old dead tree. A nice residential street which was close to the Enchanted Woods. In fact, the entrance to the woods was at the end of the road. His children played in there with all their friends. His position in the police force meant he could afford a larger property further out of the town. But they all agreed that they wanted to stay close to family, friends and school. It is comfortable enough for the four of us, he thought. He knew Philomena would not have been happy living in the upmarket part of town. She liked being here and he was content. As he opened the front door, he came face to face with his son Thom who was on his way out.

'Hia, Dad. Long time no see.' He said as he sloped of to his evening class. Solomon looked at his son's departing figure and smiled. In the height of teenage fashion, all loose clothing with his jeans hanging down far too low to look comfortable. His tee shirt about six sizes too big. And although Solomon knew the trainers were new, they looked like they were ready for the charity shop or the bin. He had been the same in his youth. Teenagers the world over think they have found the meaning to life. That parents were too thick to see and knew nothing. He had been just the same but, in his day, it had been slim fit tie dye shirts and jeans fitted down to the knee where they became bell bottoms. His hair had been long, almost waist length and he wore a head band, in the vain of American Indians he watched on the television. He also eschewed shoes for a whole year, much to his parent's disgust. Thom, he noticed wore a woollen hat in all weathers, covering up his shaved head. Different but so much the same.

'Daddy.' Yelled a little voice. Polly threw herself at her father, almost knocking him over, but he managed to pick her up and was rewarded with a smacking great chocolatey kiss.

'Hello, my darling,' he said, 'Have you been a good girl for Mummy?'

'Of courth,' she lisped. Having no front teeth. 'I've made you a pie. Mummy ith cooking it now.'
Putting down his brief case he closed the door and carried his daughter through to the kitchen. He kissed his wife and said, 'So, how are my two favourite blonds then?'

'We are good, and so pleased to see you home.' Philomena answered. 'Polly, do you think you can put your father down for a minute?'

'Thilly mummy,' she answered wriggling down out of Sol's arms. 'I can't lift Daddy, can I?'

'You just missed Thom.' Phil told him.

'No, I caught him on the door step. He is off to class?'

'Yes, he has Upland English tonight. He says it will come in handy and help with his degree. I really don't like the idea of him studying Upland languages, but he says that's where the future is.'

'Well, he can be whatever he wants to be. But I would advise against the police force. But maybe that's just because I am tired.'

'Well have a cup of tea and a piece of this lovely cherry pie Polly made,' she said with a grin that spoke volumes in conspiracy.

'Oh, how lovely. Well done Polly, it looks lovely and brown on top.' He said eyeing the burnt offering

'Yeth, twy some Daddy.' Polly said. I' I worked the pathry jutht as Mummy doeth. Wiv the woling pin.'

'And did you wash your hands?'

'UMMM well I gave then a wince.'

'Very good,' he said looking at his wife.

'Why don't you go and get into your pyjamas and you can sit with Daddy to watch your programs before bed?' her Mum suggested.

'Okay.' She said skipping up the stairs.

'Is it safe to eat?' He whispered.

'No, I'll cut a slice, and smear a plate with it. You can say how delicious it was when she comes down.' Phil told him.

'Good, shall I take my tea into the lounge? I'll put the telly on.'

'I'll be through in a moment.' Phil told him as she cut the pie, with difficulty and smeared some on a plate before throwing the rest out in the dustbin outside. She knew Polly would never go near the dustbin so would not know that her father had not eaten all the pie.

'Greedy Daddy, you've eaten it all.' Polly resplendent in pink frilly Fairy pyjamas said as she came into the lounge to take her seat on her father's lap.

'It was so scrumptious I just couldn't help myself.' He told her as she settled to watch her favourite programs.

'But you didn't have any cuthtard with it.'

'No, I just wanted to enjoy the full flavour of the pie.'

As Phil wandered into the room some time later, she found them both fast asleep. Lifting Polly up she carried the child to bed. Tucking her in and kissing her goodnight. Leaving a night light on she closed the door and went back down to her husband, who by now was awake and had switched the channel to watch the news.

'It's all about the murder. How is the investigation going?' she asked.

'Very slowly, but there is an anomaly in the accounts of Infracom that we are investigating. An unknown person has been buying shares, lots of them and recently a large deposit of shares has changed hands. This gives this person a very big holding in the company. We need to find out who that is. I don't know why it's important, we are scrabbling in the dark here. But anyone with however slight a connection to the Wicked step mother is being investigated.'

'You have discounted the immediate family? You said they all had motive.'

'Yes, motive but not the opportunity. This was ancient magic. It looks as if the woman was crushed by Walking trees.'

'Magic, but who uses magic these days?' I know there are industries that are still allowed to use it, health and such like but it's been outlawed for individuals for centuries.'

'Indeed it has, which means that not many know how to use it.'

'Fairy Godmother?'

'I've been to see her. She told me of the Walking trees spell. But it is an ancient one. She of course can be said to have a motive and the opportunity, and she is still under investigation. But I don't think it is her. I am drawn to this financial aspect. The shares disappearing from that company.'

'What draws you to them?'

'I don't know really, but I have a feeling it's significant.'

'But you don't know yet, who this person is?'

'No.' he said with a sigh. 'But we will find out.'

'Follow your instincts. It's always done you well so far.'

'Yes, but it's so good to have a night off. And to be able to discuss it with you. You always make me feel better. Thank you my darling.'

'Hia.' Called a voice from the door way.
Thom had arrived home, so his parents ended their discussion.

Solomon didn't sleep well, despite the comfort of his own bed. He still puzzled about the case. That person with the shareholding, he couldn't get out of his mind. There must be something there. But how to find out who and what?

When he did get up Phil had been up cooking him a fine breakfast. It's funny how her cooking gave him so much more energy when he needed it. Magic? Could be but he knew it was innocuous stuff. Philomena didn't hold with magic.

Chapter 15

'Anything new come in overnight, sergeant?' he asked as he entered the police station.

'I believe there has emerged some further information about the shareholding sir. I'll get Constable Perring to explain it all to you.'

'Very good,'
He settled at his desk and sifted through some reports that had been put there for him to read. Nothing new in any of those.
Constable Perring knocked and entered.

'Sit down Constable, what have you got?'

'We have located all the shareholder's sir, and I have listed them for you with their respective holdings. There is a name for the anonymous share holder but, needless to say it is fictitious. There is quite a trail we have found already with deposits coming in from worldwide. Upworld mainly. Which leads us to a problem. They are not being very helpful. Their banks say they have no compunction to provide is with any information.'

'What name do we have for the ghost share holder then?' Crumb asked sighing.

'The only name we have found to date is Pearl Loin.'

'Pearl Loin? As in purloin to steal?'

Shaking his head in disbelief D. C. I. Crumb felt all the energy drain out of him.

'Yes sir.'

'Keep at it then Constable. Get a team together. We need to find out who this is.'

'Yes sir.' Constable Perring left the room.

'Oh, good god.' Solomon groaned. And continued looking through the reports. He remembered his conversation with his wife the previous evening. He had said that everyone who had motive did not have the opportunity. But he now realised that there was one person in the palace who did have that opportunity. Away in her dream world, the only person who could not account for their movements always was the Queen. Could he? Should he? He looked at his phone and it knew who he wanted to talk to.

'Droove here.'

'Ahh, inspector. Can I have a word?'

'Yes, sir. On my way.'

The Inspector knocked and entered.

'Sit down, this is a bit awkward, but I think It must be done.'

'Sir?'

'I need you to put the Queen under surveillance.'

'You suspect the Queen? Or eliminating?'

'Neither at this point, but when she goes walk about, she is nowhere that can be verified. As such she had no alibi.'

'I can see the need to eliminate her, it will be interesting to see where she goes.'

'No need within the palace, her movements there are well documented, but outside she is a misnomer.'

'I'll see to it sir. Imps would be best for this job, I think. Us poor Goblins are a bit clumsy and not good for undercover work.'

'Yes, they would be good, see if there are any volunteers in the Imp force. Don't want to force anyone to take on such a task.'

'Right you are,' Droove said as he left the room.

Crumb settled back in his chair and thought that he had one other aspect covered. He had to get on to the deployment of the forces to police the crowds that will be going to view the wedding procession. At Least they would not be going far. The cathedral is only half a mile from the palace. And most of the journeys are being taken in shielded cars. The carriage that the Sisters were travelling in was a different matter. He needed to have another word with the Fairy Godmother about that. Just to make sure when she conjured it up, she put protection in the spell. He could remember signing the request for the use of that spell and had meant to mention it at the time. There would need to be a police presence at the media boxes as well. Not that he expected any trouble, but keen fairies would like to get to a better position to see the coach pass. They may climb up the structures for a better vantage point. He hoped he wouldn't need to take any officers off the murder investigation. Ideally, he would love to get it all tied up prior to the wedding but that looked less likely with every passing day.

Chapter 16

The King arrived at Hardwick Manor. He was greeted by a perplexed Baron.

'Your Majesty. It is good of you to grace my humble home with your presence.'

'Please don't stand on ceremony, Brian, I have come to visit you as a friend. We have known each other a long while. May I sit here?' The King said indicating a comfortable chair near the fire.

'Of course Sir.' Replied the Baron sitting in the chair opposite.

'Brian, we have been in touch with Upworld funeral directors. Not something we are very familiar with, funerals. I just wondered how you wanted to proceed.'

'I have given it much thought, Sir. But have not come up with an answer. I have been reading up on it though. Do we bury her or cremate her? I don't know which way to go. Or we could build a funeral Pyre and place her on top?' I don't want a big affair, very private if possible. Probably after the wedding or maybe before would be better? I just don't know.'

'Have the police indicated when they will be able to release the body?'

'It, she can come home any time now. They have all the information they need I think.'

'Well, my dear chap, to either bury or cremate is your choice. They have her being kept cold at the forensic labs, so it can be before or after the wedding.'

'It may be better before if possible, then the girls will not have to think about it all during their honeymoons. I think cremate. '

'Where would you like the service?'

'My wife didn't attend any church, I'm not sure she had any religion that is practised these days, so could it be here? Something else I would need to look into.'

'If that is what you want, we will probably need a permit. I shall speak to Crumb if you like.'

'Oh, the Detective Chief Inspector. Yes, I expect he will have to sign something to allow it.'

The King nodded sadly, he felt sorry for his old friend. Such a terrible thing to happen. And now he was faced with an almost unheard-of ceremony. No one knew how to conduct such a service. He would ring Crumb and organize the body to be brought home. This had to be sorted if the funeral was to be prior to the wedding. As there were only a few days before guests began to arrive, they had better be getting on with it.

'Just let me know when you want to do it and I will get my secretary onto the arrangements.'

The Baron stood and paced the room. Then as if putting a steel bar up his back he straightened and said. 'Three days from now. Let's get it done and then concentrate on the wedding. In three days, I will say goodbye and begin a new life. Metaphorically speaking.' He smiled at the King.

That's more like my dear friend, the King thought. He has been missing lately. But his decisiveness has returned.

'I will speak to the girls and Ella, we will get together here at 2 o'clock and burn my old life.'

'So be it, I will speak with the Queen and the Prince and we will be here for that time.'

'Thank you, your Highness.'
The King stood and shook the Baron's hand, he turned and left as he saw tears in his friend's eyes. Knowing what a private man he was with his emotions the King didn't want to stay and embarrass the Baron.
As he left the Manor, he heard the Baron break down and cry.

So, it was that three days later a small gathering at the Manor witnessed the funeral pyre of the Wicked step mother. The Baron had discussed with some Upworld funeral directors who all expressed the difficulty of building a coffin to accommodate a flat body. They asked if Pyre would be possible and so the Baron further consulted with the Detective Chief Inspector who was signing off the permit.

'Yes, there is no reason why you should not have a Pyre. Just take safety into consideration. Make sure it isn't too close to the house. Maybe on the lake? I have heard that Upworld Countries do that sometimes, but on the sea?'

'Thank you, yes I have read of such funerals. I will get the pyre built and you will have her escorted here?'

'Of course. Is it alright if I attend? I have heard it is something Upworld police do for such a death.'

'Murder you mean. You will be very welcome.'

In attendance around the pyre were Cinderella and her Prince both of whom kept a dignified but hard look on their faces. Crying in public was not considered correct behaviour for Royalty. As he watched her Crumb could see that Princes Ella was holding back real tears. The King with the Queen who looked resplendent, sober and alert. The D. C. I. had never seen her sober, holding a normal conversation, able to stand without help and able to concentrate on the service without zoning out. He felt even more sure that he was doing the right thing by having the surveillance on her.

Esme was standing hand in hand with Richard. Gris, standing beside Stuart who had a protective arm around her. The girls were shedding quiet gentle tears. The Manor servants who were in a group with Buttons and Dan, had come for the Baron's sake to pay their respects. The D. C. I. along with Inspector Droove. Of course, the Baron who was to light the fire and the Fairy Godmother. The question of how to get her up on the pyre was solved by a bit of levitation performed by the Fairy Godmother. She pointed her wand at the flattened body of Madeline Hardwick and levitated her gently up and draped her over the fire. At a given moment Baron Hardwick put a flame to the pile.

The Fairy Godmother had warned everyone that Madeline was likely to make a noise. To say her goodbyes to this world and enter the afterlife but the sound when it came was and ear-piercing, ear drum bursting, blood bubbling full throated guttural scream, which made the hairs stand up on everyone's arms. The sound carried on upwards until it was too far away to be heard. The smoke burst into a rainbow of colour and light with bangs, whistles and whooshing sounds. The display would not have disgraced the most expensive firework display. Everyone was enthralled but they would never be able to enjoy a firework display again without thinking of this day. Is that her legacy? One last spoiler? The Fairy Godmother thought to herself.

Chapter 17

After the gathering had partaken of some light refreshments, they all departed to leave the family in peace. The Fairy Godmother approached Crumb. 'Sorry to bother you but I was just wondering how the investigation was going?'

 'Slowly Ma-am. We may have need of your expertise again if that is acceptable.'

'Any time inspector just have the thought and I can make time.'

'You don't want to make an appointment?' Inspector Droove cut in.

'Inspector, that will not be necessary.' She smiled at his naivety. Obviously, he didn't pay attention to his magic history lessons in school, she thought.

'Thank you, Ma-am,' Solomon said. And they made their way to the waiting car.

As the two policemen settled in and after Solomon instructed the vehicle where to take them, he turned to Droove and asked. 'Well what did you think of that?'

'It's a first for me, never been to a funeral before. What a racket, really put the spooks up me. Who would have thought she could make such a noise after death? Was she that loud when she was alive?'

'Probably. But I didn't gain any insight in the gathering. No acting there. But did you notice the

Queen? She was sober and showed no sign of alcohol abuse.'

'Pretty amazing how she can shake it off when she needs to.'

'My thoughts exactly. Keep up with the surveillance.'

'My Imps are on to it. I'll let you have their first report when it has been typed up.'

'Not their forte, typing is it? Nor writing for that matter, they can't stay still long enough.'

'No but they are fantastic at going about unobserved. Got to hand it to them.'

'Can't argue with that.'

Solomon went directly to his office to read any further reports that may have come regarding the investigation. Also to finalise the arrangements for policing the wedding. That all seemed to be in hand. There was one report from the constable who was looking into the financial aspect. They had found a further bank account linked to Pearl Loin. This one was an Infraworld bank and they supplied good information regarding when the account was opened. They even supplied the copies of proof of identity. A Tax bill and photo license of a young woman with long blond hair. She looked very similar to Cinderella. The name on the account was Ali Mynne. All Mine? This person was having a good old joke at the expense of the banks. Or even at our expense?

A knock on the door and Alex Droove entered with the first report from the Imps.

'Good, thanks. Look at this.' He handed over the bank reports.

'Whoever this is, he is having a laugh.' Alex sighed.

'May have nothing to do with the murder but we need to follow this up. Put some more staff on to it. We need to find out who this is, I feel it is important. Now what have the Imps got to say?'

'She wanders in to the Enchanted Woods and once out of sight of the palace stands up straight Walking briskly to the same clearing each time. There she is enveloped by a shrub. It looks just like any innocuous shrub but on closer investigation they discovered it is a door. She will stay there for just few minutes and then make her way back to the palace, assuming the stoop and stumble when in sight of the windows again.'

'We need to find where that door leads to. She isn't just popping in there to relieve herself, is she? There is something in there.'

'Already on to it. I will get a bigger team together to look into these accounts.'

'Good, thanks Alex.'

Solomon sighed again. He could do with a drink of something very noxious. But he had given all that up. Never good for the health or the brain power. But the desire had never left him. He supposed that once addicted the habit would stay with you and resisting didn't get any easier as time went by. He hoped Thom never dabbled. And little Polly. He knew it was no good pointing out the dangers to teenagers it just made it more desirable to them. All the talks he did in schools following the acceptable teaching standards were, he knew, about as much use a chocolate fire guard. New substances were hitting the streets all the time, more powerful and dangerous than what he had ever used. He had been able to stop before he totally ruined his own life and he had Philomena to thank for that. He looked at his desk phone and thought of his wife.

'Hello Solly, are you home tonight? I'll make something nice. Not one of Polly's pies, I promise

'Yes, I'll be home before Polly's bed time. Just make sure there is plenty of cuthtard.'

'Stop Taking the mickey out of her lisp. She will get teeth soon enough.' She said laughing.

Smiling he cut the call.

Chapter 18

The Fairy Godmother made her own way back to her shop. She had a feeling that the D. C. I. would be visiting soon. She knew she would have to find answers to his questions. Had the murderer been magical? But where and how? She had contacts all over and her own enquiries had come to nothing. It must be someone local. She only knew of two who could possibly execute such a spell. The Queen, and the Upworlder she had been instructing in magic language. She knew he had more knowledge than he would admit to, but could he be that powerful? You can never tell with Upworlders. They had eschewed magic for hundreds of years and seemed to be able to get along very nicely without it. She didn't know if she should try and find a way of sharing this information with the D. C. I.

To do so would put her in great danger. He would know who had informed on him, and would be within his rights to take revenge, according to ancient laws. This was a quandary and no mistake. But the Queen, she was very disturbed at the thought of the cancelled wedding, with good reason. She had been determined to confront the Wicked step mother. Would they consider that she had lost control? Maybe used a spell that went wrong? She knew the D. C. I. was having the

Queen followed. Those Imps are good but not clever enough to fool the Fairy Godmother.

No, she didn't think the Queen could be accused of this crime. She reasoned that there were others that had been very angry, but could they have the power to cast such a spell. No, this magic was beyond the average story Fairy . She didn't like to think the Queen would be a suspect, but just because you like someone, she thought, that is no reason to discount them.

The wedding preparations could now take priority in every body's minds. Having got the funeral out of the way the King could concentrate on the arrangements for the visitors who were due to start arriving any time. There was to be a ball as soon as everyone was assembled. He had a definitive list now of all those who had put aside their fears and decided to attend. It was a copy of the list that had been made before the murder, but he knew that those coming were all friends.

Mainly it had ended up with Fairy Story characters and a few Royal families from other spirit worlds. The Goblins King, the Elf Queen. They would be accommodated in the palace. The characters of Snow White were coming and all staying in one of the new hotels. Sleeping beauty and their retinue also had accepted. The Wicked Witch had been distraught at the death of the Step Mother but was able to attend. She would have her own security.

Red Riding Hood also had accepted and having put aside their fears all the other characters in that story would bring their own accommodation. Many hundreds were attending the ceremony but had not felt able to stay, still being nervous. Well, not such a big celebration as he had first thought but there would be enough to give the Baron's daughters a good send off. Perhaps that would make up to Cinderella for not allowing her and Charles to have a state wedding. All this to appease his daughter in law.

Cinderella, for her part was rushing now to get the dresses finished. There were not just the wedding dresses but ball gowns for the banquet, going away outfits for the brides. Her own dress and ball gown. She had several ideas about her own but felt she should try and play down her costumes. After all it would not do to outshine the brides.

Her work force of hard-working fairies was tired. She knew they needed a rest, but she really needed to get on with the London Fashion week entries.

On entering the vast work room, she called attention of the fairies.

'Ladies and gentlemen, may I please have your attention. I want to thank you all for your hard work. Without your conscientious labour we would never have been ready. As you know we will be putting entries into London Fashion week. But prior to that you all need some rest and relaxation. To this end you all have two weeks leave as soon as the wedding outfits are finished to satisfaction of our customers.'

The cheer that emitted from that factory could be heard as far away as the palace. They got back to work with renewed vigour. It always helps to keep the workforce happy, she thought.

 The Queen back in her apartments looking for all the world as if she had a really bad day, decided she had to get out. So, putting on her cloak she left the palace by her usual exit. The Imps following were alert and ready, they knew the funeral would be upsetting. She would be likely to go walk about. But who was that also following her.

An Upworlder. The two Imps split up and with one continuing to follow the Queen the other went with the Upworlder. The Upworlder was good. He darted about all over the place and even the practised Imp had trouble keeping him in sight. But eventually he stopped at the very bush the Queen went to and turning three times he disappeared. The Imp knew this was an old Upworlder invisibility spell. Strange man, why would he be following the Queen visible and then turn invisible? Why not tail her while he was invisible? Must tell the inspector about this.

Chapter 19

The ball was a great success. Everyone had enjoyed the evening. Baron Hardwick was offered a seat at the top table with the Queen on his right. She had been in good form. She didn't touch any gin, did have a couple of glasses of wine which didn't affect her at all. She had joked and kept up the conversation. No mention of his wife at all. The assembled company had obviously put her from their minds. The Baron did notice that she was staring at someone in the lower quadrant of the ball room. A small sigh could be heard from her every now and then, but she shook herself and carried on with animated and topical conversation. The King was happy to see his wife behaving in such a way and privately thanked her for making such an effort.

'My dear, I am enjoying this. We should have more banquets, more fun. Life is so hard and such a slog. We should party more.' She leaned over and told him.

'If that would help to make you happy, we can do that within reason. They are very expensive to hold.'

'Always the money, lighten up. We can always make more. There are thousands of antiques in the palace we could sell to Upworld.'

'My dear, you may have something there. Perhaps you will accompany me to the attics tomorrow and look to see if we can dispose of some of them.' The King said, not only thinking this a superb idea but it was something he may be able to engage the Queen's interest in. Give her something to hold her attention to, a light at the end of a very long tunnel?

'Time for dancing, clear the tables.' The Queen called. She was keen to dance and be near Raphael. Within seconds the tables had been cleared and put away, the orchestra tuned up and the dancing started. Dance cards were soon filled, and all the assembled began to energetically work off the calories they had consumed. One couple present declined to dance as they simply were not very good at it. Solomon and Philomena. This kind of dancing was not to Goblins' taste. Philomena had been enthralled to receive the invitation and had spent a fortune on one of Ella's designer dresses. But she looked gorgeous, Solomon thought to himself and was very proud of his wife. With her on his arm they wandered around the ball room talking and chatting with all the other guests.

'No shop talking tonight.' she had ordered him.

'Deal' he answered. But he couldn't help but keep a look out for any untoward activity. He is a policeman at the end of the day. He had already noted that this was the second time he had seen the Queen behaving as a Queen is expected to act. He couldn't help but think how different she was when in public to the drunken wandering gin-soaked shell of the Fairy she showed most days. But he also suspected now that was a ruse. Why, he wondered. Could she be the killer? Could she have murdered the Step Mother?

He did notice that she had danced with the wood man at least twice. What was it about him? A lowly born man? Were they old friends?

'This is a slow one, we could shuffle to this without making fools of ourselves.' Phil said grabbing his arm and dragging him onto the dance floor. He noticed that she had pushed through the dancing throng to stop near the Queen to shuffle. Clever girl. But it was no good, they were talking in a foreign language. Shame Thom wasn't here. He, with his propensity for foreign tongues may have been able to decipher what they were saying.

'Good try my love.' he said to his wife. 'But I thought you said no shop tonight.'

'However else was I going to get your full attention?'

'Fair enough. My fair lady will you dance with me?'

'Oh, kind sir, I would be enamoured. Not the right word is it?'

Laughing he said. 'Probably not, but it will do for me,'

'No glass slipper tonight?' Charley asked Ella.

'God no, do you know how much those things hurt my feet? The suffering I went through to catch you is unheard of.'

'Oh, my poor dear. But am I worth all that pain?'

'Let me get back to you on that.' She said laughing. Esme and Richard were in a close clinch. 'Wedding next and when we get back can we hold a ball in our new house? When it's ready that is?'

'If you want to hold a ball my dearest, you certainly can. You have no need to ask, it will be as much your house as mine you know. Just let me know the dates so I can diarize it.'

Diarize? Whatever sort of word is that. You going all American on me? You mean put it in your diary, don't you?'

'Yes, Okay. You just tell me the dates, better still I will give you my diary and you can fill in the dates I must be dressed up.' He said ending the conversation with a kiss. Gris and Stuart had slipped out of the room on to the balcony to look at the stars.

'Do you think Mum is up there somewhere? Looking down on us being so happy?'

'I think she may let us know if she was,' he answered. 'But would she have been happy for us? The next big do is our wedding, and all these people are here for that.'

'Yes, we have a lot to thank Ella for. Still keeping where we are going a secret?'

'My lips are sealed. I'm not saying but you will find out when you get there.'

'Plane? Ship? Train? Or just plain old coach.'

'Shush, you will find out soon enough.' He said quietening her with a kiss.
The King and Baron Hardwick were sitting together watching all the dancing couples.

'The Queen seems happy tonight.'

'Yes, she always did love a party. We need to have more, and more fun all around. I was thinking of Taking her away for a holiday after the wedding. I wonder if she would like to visit some of the Upworld.'

'Well, it would not be a holiday unless you travel incognito. If you go as King and Queen, it will be state visits all over the place.'

'I had wondered about that. I will have to have a word with Charley and Ella. They have been. And of course, they will be going again in September.' They are planning a longer stay in London and Taking the children as well. How things have changed. Time was when it was impossible to travel between the two worlds in safety. Only very brave or foolish Fairy 's would venture to Upworld.'

'And how many of them returned unscathed?'

'Yes, very different now. We must keep up with the times. I was thinking about us forming the parliament. The King and Queen are figure heads and bring in tourists. They do good work and are kept busy but don't have the worry of the state of their nation. That is in the hand of the government. At Least in Britain they do. I have been studying it all.'

'It is an interesting concept. Would it really work here do you think?'

'I've had some studies done to see the viability of it, as we discussed at the conference. Many would like to see the end of the monarchy just as many in Upworld do. I would like to visit the parliaments in some of those countries to learn how they work. I have thought about it long and hard, being King is such an onerous task I could do with some help.'

'But Charles takes what he can from you doesn't he?'

'The dear boy does what he can, but we are facing challenging times and I think we need to move on. I have spoken to him and he is as keen as I am. It's just as well we managed to get the rest of the Lords to agree.'

'Well, let me know if there is anything I can do. Meanwhile, If you are agreeable, I shall retire to my home for the rest of the evening. Some quiet time before the girls break my peace.'

'Of course, my friend. Good night.'

As the Baron left the palace, he spotted the Queen Walking at speed down one of the long corridors. She had her cloak on and looked as if she was stepping outdoors.

At midnight the Fairy Godmother appeared to wish all present a good night and the party broke up. The King went in search of the Queen. He found her in her apartments dressed for bed and drunk. Sadly, shaking his head, he left her and went to his own bed.

Chapter 20

The day at last dawned. This was it. The day that all the preparation culminated in. The Wedding. Ella had been at the Manor house at the crack of dawn with an army of dressers, hair dressers and make-up artists to make the Ugly sisters look beautiful for their Grooms and their big day.

Esme was in tears, her mother was missing it all. Ella hugged her and that started Gris off. So, she had a hug as well. 'Enough now. You will spoil your make up.' She told them. And the preparations of the brides began. Two each of the girls' friends were to be bridesmaids. They were being dressed in another room and Ella's fairies were busy working on them. In yet another room Ella's oldest children Edward and Andrew were preparing for their job as ring carriers. Their cushions the exact colour in fact made from the same material as the bridesmaid's dresses.

'It's a good job the aisle of the cathedral is extra wide, so you can both walk up together.' She said thoughtfully.

'Yes, I can't have her arriving at the alter before me.' Esme said with a wicked smile on her face.

'Oh ho, we will see about that.' Gris answered. And the challenge was on apparently.

'No! You will give the poor organist a heart attack if you don't walk in time to the music.' Ella laughed. 'And think of Father, trying to keep up with you two.'
The preparation hours were slipping away from them and by the time the girls, their friends and the ring boys were ready Ella realised she had no time to change herself. Thank goodness for the Fairy Godmother who arrived with the coach. One wave of her wand and Ella was dressed and ready.
With a wicked smile the Godmother said. 'Bring back any memories? My dear.'

 Ella ushered the bridesmaids and ring boys into waiting cars and then went to make sure her father was ready. He was in his parlour having a quick brandy to settle his nerves but was ready to do his duty to his step daughters. She kissed him and left in her own car to meet them all at the cathedral.

Six white horses pulled the carriage which was shaped like a pumpkin. As they left the Manor, they saw the roads lined with crowds waving and cheering. 'Oh, I feel like royalty', Esme said waving back to them. All the way to the cathedral there were crowds, and outside where the guests had arrived there was a huge crowd. They had all gathered to see the beings they had lived their lives reading about and telling their children stories about. All too soon the Brides arrived at the cathedral and alighted from their coach. Once they were safely on the ground and had adjusted the frocks the coach disappeared. Poof! It was gone.

'Well where would they park it?' The Baron said to his daughters surprised faces. 'Ready'?

At the nod he stood between them and spread his arms, so they could take one each.

'Let's go then, shall we girls?' After all the upset, the preparations, the dress fittings, decisions. Death of their mother, her funeral, the investigations and everything the day was here, and they were Walking down the aisle to meet their husbands to be. They walked in time to the music.

Must be the first time in their lives they had followed instructions. Ella saw the smile on each face and wondered if they had something planned. But they just looked at her in all innocence as they made their sedate way to the alter where they were to take their vows.

The King had taken Ella aside and said that he needed a few minutes with the boys before the wedding vows were exchanged. 'Privately?' she asked.

'No, better in public. I was always going to do this and it's just a shame I didn't get a chance to tell your step mother of my plans.'

When all were assembled, and the brides were in place he stepped out and stood in front of the couples. Taking his sword out of its scabbard he tapped each of the young men on the shoulder and conferred knighthoods on them for their services to industry. Now they had titles and Madeline had got herself in a temper for nothing. If only he had been able to tell her before she went stumbling into the Enchanted Woods. My timing has always been a bit suspect he thought to himself.

Ella noticed that the word 'obey' had been removed for the vows. She nodded knowing it would have been a lie anyway.

On their way out of the cathedral the girls couldn't resist the challenge and ran out, barging each other until they reached the big oak door. Their poor husbands left behind to watch their wives disappear. But when they arrived at the door they stopped and stepped out together. Never one in front, never one behind. That had been their saying as children and so it was now.

They waited for their husbands to catch up and waved at the cheering crowds. Shrinking back when they saw the Fairy Godmother standing just outside with her arms folded looking for all the world as if she was going to explode. But she smiled at them. 'It's your day my dears and if you want to behave like brats you can.' She said kissing them each on the cheek.

The Queen was in good spirits, her day had come at last, she didn't know how she was going to hold in her excitement. The planning that had gone into this day. The fear and nerves all but forgotten. Tonight, she would be back in her own story. With the love of her life. Her wood-man. But first she had to endure the ball. To sit beside the King and watch as speeches were orated, as food was eaten and presents given and the cake had been cut. That was her time to slip away, when everybody was occupied watching the two happy

119

couples carrying out this tradition. But she could wait.
She had waited this long and another few hours would
be nothing.

But when the time came, she found it difficult to slide
off. The King was so close to her side. Only one thing for
it. And she popped some drops before ordering a large
gin and tonic. She could see the alarm on the King's
face but knew he would not stand beside her if she was
drunk. For the sake of his good name and because he
could not stand to be with her when she was in her
cups. She felt him move away and speak to Charles.

'What can we do?' Charles asked him, 'she will take
herself off soon. She never likes to be in company when
she is drunk.'

'Well we just have to hope she goes before she
embarrasses herself.'
Downing her drink, she started to go into her pretence
and stood unsteadily. She weaved her way to the door
glancing to make sure she had not been noticed by
many of the assembled crowd.

'I'll just go and make sure she gets back to her
apartment safely.' The King told his son.

'I'll hold court here and perhaps you two won't be
noticed by your absence.' Charles answered going in
search of Ella, who he needed by his side right now.

The King slipped out and made his way toward the
Queens apartments. As he entered, he found the Fairy
Godmother there as well, thinking she had also come to
check Sophia was alright he was gratified at her
presence. But where was the Queen? Then he saw her,

in the arms of the wood man. Dressed as a simple woodland wife.

'I'm going.' She told him. 'Don't try to stop me, please don't.'

'You are not drunk then. I thought you had downed a couple of doubles there.'

'I have never been drunk. How do you think I knew exactly what went on in this palace? By pretending to be drunk, people wouldn't even lower their voices when they saw me. I knew all the gossip. Everything.' She told him, accusingly. 'But you only saw what you wanted to see. A drunken sop of a wife. But I have been planning this for eons.'

'So now you tell me this after a lifetime of worrying about you? Now you want to go? After all this time?'

'After all this time. I have waited too long. Now at last I can think of my own happiness.'

'I grew to love you, I protected you. We have a son who needs his mother nearby.'

'He is a grown man with his own family. He doesn't need me. You don't need me. I will never make you happy. I have lived this lie for too long. I don't belong here, the reason I was brought here is now past. The two tribes have integrated and even interbred. I am not needed here any longer. If you love me as you say, you will let me go.'

Like a broken man the King sunk into a chair. He looked at his wife's beautiful face looking so much younger with a smile. The joy he saw there radiating from her. As she held the hand of the wood man.

121

Raphael, that's his name the King thought. How long since he had thought of him? He wondered. But he couldn't deny his wife her happiness any longer. He knew he had lost her. Well, never had her love, anyway did he? She had been forced into this marriage and he knew he had to let her go. He nodded and found the strength to stand up.

Holding out his hand to the wood man he said. 'I hope you can do what I could never do. Make her happy.' And they shook hands. Then as the two lovers stepped backwards into a stream of light she turned to the King.

'I didn't do it, you know. I didn't kill her.' And those were the last words he ever heard from his Queen. The Fairy Godmother waved her wand and they were gone.

'She had wanted to go many times before this.' The Fairy Godmother told him.

'Is that why she was so disgruntled when I refused a state wedding for the Prince? Would she have gone then?'

'Yes, she needed Raphael here to enable her to cross the divide. She couldn't go on her own, he had to accompany her back to her own story.'

'I will miss her. As bad as things were between us, I will miss her.'

'Yes, but now we must get back to the celebrations. And you must put on a brave face.'

'Oh, not yet, I need a few moments. Please have someone come and fetch me when the happy couples depart. Can I just stay here for a few moments?'

'I will be back. Don't dwell on it too long. She has gone, and you must carry on.'

'I never thought she had killed Madeline Hardwick, did you?'

'Momentarily, yes. I had suspicions, but she doesn't tell lies and she said she didn't do it.'

'Doesn't tell lies? Her whole life here has been a lie. Or a pretence anyway.'

'True, but I believe her, why would she lie now? When she knew she was safe and out of it all back in her own story.'

'I don't know, I don't understand any of it.' He said sitting down in his wife's favourite chair.'

The Fairy Godmother went back down to the ball, she drew Ella and Charlie aside and Taking them into a side room told them what had happened. In shock and so stunned by the revelation that they also both needed to sit down. How could this be?

'On a simply practical note, how did she manage it? How could she look so drunk and incapable but still be sober and learn the magic she needed to do this?' Ella asked.

'Why?' Charley also asked.

'We can discuss it all when the ball is over, and all the guests have gone. I will tell you everything I know at that point. But suffice to say, she has some magic.'

'Ha, not just a simple wood man's wife then?' Charley said with bitterness creeping into his voice.

'All will be answered but you have to be bold now and face your guests. I believe the happy couples are departing. I'll fetch your Father.'

Everyone was gathered on the high staircase that led up to the main front door of the palace. Down in the drive way beside each other were two brand new shiny Upworld Rolls Royce cars. The girls both threw they bouquets over their shoulders and one was caught by the Baron, who immediately shoved it into the arms of the person standing beside him. One of the Queens waiting ladies. She blushed and curtsied. The other was caught by the King who immediately threw it over his shoulder. Unable to stop himself he turned to see who had caught it and looked directly into the eyes of the most beautiful woman he had ever seen. He didn't know who she was but good God she was a stunner. He thought he should try and find out just who she was.

And they were off. Both cars driving slowly down the long curving drive way still side by side, and at the gate they turned in opposite directions. The Fairy Godmother knew they were going to expensive resort islands. She also knew that these islands were owned by the two Prentiss Brothers. Those boys had done well. There is something behind all that, I know there is, she said to herself.

The Ball went on into the early hours and then all the guests departed for their respective accommodation. The King asked the Fairy Godmother if she would make her way to his apartments if she was not too tired.

'Of course, I'm not tired, she said. Sleep is overrated anyway.' There were lots of questions the King, Charles and Ella wanted to ask. She knew they would want answers and now she knew that they deserved the whole truth.

Chapter 21

The three of them made themselves as comfortable as possible and waited for the Fairy Godmother to arrive. When she walked in, she went to sit in the only available chair and started to talk.

'Sophia came to me soon after Ella and Charles met. She wanted me to try to make you give them a state wedding, your highness. But to no avail. You were adamant.'

'To my great regret, I know you, Charles were very disappointed at my decision. And I want to say right now that I am sorry.'

'You didn't think Ella was good enough to become a princess. I was angry and upset at the time and it still hurts but that is all years ago and we have moved on.'

'The Queen wanted the state wedding then for the same reason that she was so pleased to see this one. She knew that the laws regarding story hopping were very strict and she needed Raphael here to escort her back to her own story. She could not just go. She had been working with lawyers for years to find a way around the problem. But Raphael needed to be invited here and then he could take her back.' The Fairy Godmother said.

'You see, she had never wanted to come here. Our marriage was a political move to heal the differences between certain factions. I had to marry a commoner and she had to rise to the rank of Queen. She didn't come freely, she was forced.' Added the King.

'Well, it is easy to see that she wasn't happy here. Gin was her only solace?' Charles said.

'She was never drunk, she was Taking drops I made for her to immunize herself from the alcohol. She just acted drunk. She came to me and told me what she wanted to do, and I made the drops up for her. I didn't like doing it, but she was prepared to use her own magic if I didn't. I have been teaching her some small spells and have been the only friend she had for many years.'

'What? Never drunk? It was all an act?' Both Ella and Charles were shocked.

'All of it, I only found out earlier today. As her husband I should have known, she hid it all so well.' The King told them.

'She was planning to go just as soon as this Raphael was invited here? What if he had not been on the guest list?' Charles asked.

'She made sure he was.' The Fairy Godmother said.

'She used magic?' Ella spoke at last.

'I think so. It didn't occur to me to invite him, but his name was there.' The King said to them.

'Then my mother said she was going to cancel the wedding. The Queen didn't seem phased by that. But she must have been very angry. I don't want to think like this, but do you think she ....'

'No. she said she didn't do it, and I believe her.' Insisted the King.

'I believe her as well.' The Fairy Godmother added. Unconvinced Ella pointed out that the woman was not one they really knew. She had lied to them all these years and had upped and left. How could they be sure she didn't murder the step mother?

'I have had my suspicions, but I don't think she would have gone to such drastic lengths as that. There was someone else however had reason to be very annoyed at the cancellation of the wedding, who comes to mind. He is an Upworlder and I feel I need to look further into him. He has been coming to me for a while and wanting to know the ancient language.'

'Is it anyone we might know?' Ella asked.

'No, my dear but he does know your two brothers in law. But right now, we must discuss how we give out the news of the Queens disappearance. The guests will not expect to see her again as they all witnessed her leaving the Ball Room in a state. When they have all gone The King needs to put out a statement.'

'Yes, I suppose I must. But I have to inform Crumb first thing.'

Solomon arrived home two days after the wedding to a lavish meal prepared by his wife. He had stayed to oversee the clear up arrangements and make sure no crimes had taken place in the crowds, staying the night at the police station. Polly had been allowed to stay up late to greet her father and Thom had even stayed

128

home that night. Solomon was exhausted and looking forward to a lovely cosy evening with his family. The wedding day had gone well, as far as the police force was concerned. No major incidents. And the clearing up was still now Taking place. All the guests that were not staying in the palace had been escorted to where ever they were lodging. Many departed yesterday, the day following the wedding, but some had stayed to rest up but tomorrow, they would all depart. Seated at the table the family discussed the day and Polly could not stop talking about the beautiful dresses. Finally, they managed to get the over excited little girl to bed. Thom went to play on his computer.

'I can relax for a night, but back to the investigation tomorrow.'

'You've worked so hard on this case.'

'It is the biggest one we have ever dealt with in the Infraworld. Never has there been a murder of a story book character before. And with so many people having reason to get rid of her it's like looking in an ever-changing maze to find the answers.'

'Would she really have cancelled the wedding? Especially as the knighthood was already planned. That was her argument wasn't it?'

'Who knows, she isn't here to ask now is she? She was never told of the pending knighthood. The King didn't get a chance to tell her. She was killed before he could talk to her.'

'But it comes down to people who know that sort of magic, doesn't it? You still suspect the Queen?'

'She had the magic but as far as I can see she really didn't have much motive. She didn't seem bothered about the wedding one way or another, she is a consideration but not a serious one. I am looking for someone who does have that sort of magic and had a good motive.'

'The only person with that knowledge is the Fairy Godmother.'

'Yes. She is being followed as well. But she is quite elusive, not easy even for Imps to follow her.'

'Would it not be against everything she believes in though? To kill someone?'

'That is the biggest problem I have with suspecting her. We are getting closer with the forensic accounting though. The person buying all those shares in Infracom Communications has accounts all over, but the main ones are in Upworld. And we have to have a court order to look into them. The Upworld banks are not being very helpful. They have confidentiality laws they say. But I think they are just being awkward for the sake of it.'

'You feel that is where the answer lays?'

'Well, there is more to this than her throwing the toys out of her pram and annoying people. Someone really wanted this wedding to go ahead. But who had such a compelling reason that they had to kill her?'

Chapter 22

D. C. I. Crumb arrived in his office the following day and sighed as he looked at the reports on his desk. Oh well, better make a start. Just as he picked up the first one his desk phone bleeped. A small voice announced, 'The King.'

'Sir, how can I help?'

'I have something to tell you Crumb, But I wonder if you can come to the palace?'

'Of course Sir. I will come straight over.'

'I'll have my P.P.S. meet you out front, so you can get directly up here.'

'Thank you, Sir.'

As Crumb arrived at the King's office, he was ushered straight in.

'Thank you for being so prompt Detective Chief Inspector. What I have to tell you will be announced later today but I felt it important that you know first. My wife has gone. She has moved back to her own story.'

'Indeed Sir, I am sorry for your loss.'

'The reason this is significant is that she had need to wait for the wedding to enable her to go. It occurs to me that you would have been interested in that connection. She apparently needed to make sure the celebration went ahead but, I only found out myself, yesterday.'

Crumb listened to the King's explanation with a sinking feeling. One of his suspects had now disappeared. And she had even more motive than he at first thought. If she had been the perpetrator then he has lost her.

'Her own story?'

'My wife was from another faction of Fairies. We had need to bring the two tribes together. I was forced to marry a commoner from the other side and elevate her to be my Queen. She was chosen but not willingly. She has now gone back to be with the lover she had been torn away from. As he was from another story she had to wait until he could come here and escort her home.'

'So, he was invited to the wedding?'

'Yes, she made sure he was. As you can see the wedding was very important to her.'

'Indeed, she had motive to kill the Step Mother. But did she have the Magic?'

'To ascertain how much magic she had you will need to speak to the Fairy Godmother. In such a case I think she will be at liberty to speak to you.'

Taking his leave, he told his car to find the Fairy Godmother. This new innovation took some getting used too but he found it incredibly convenient. He could get on with paperwork, sit back and have a smoke, play computer games or even take a nap if he so desired while the car did all the work. Locating the Fairy Godmother had been a surprise. He expected the car to head into town but when he looked up, he was in the

Enchanted Wood. Parked by a shrub in fact. Had something gone wrong? Or had his quest not been clear enough? But just as he was about to re-programme the vehicle the Fairy Godmother emerged from the shrub.

'Inspector, I have been expecting you. Do come in.' The shrub parted the branches, and he entered the large country residence of the venerable lady.

Seated in her large lounge which was furnished in a similar way to her town house, with large windows revealing scenes of the enchanted wood. Real windows? He wondered.

'Yes inspector, they are real windows and they open so I can go Walking in the wood.'

'In perfect privacy.'

'When I have a need to be alone. Now how can I help you?'

'I find that I need to question you regarding the Queen? How much magic she had? Could she even have killed Madeline Hardwick?'

'As she has gone the King probably explained that I am now at liberty to impart information to you regarding Sophia. She did not have enough magic to be able to perform the Walking trees spell. She had only what I taught her and that is one I would never divulge.'

'So, you don't think I've let a murderer leave unpunished? If you will forgive me, I really need a bit more than your opinion. I have to be able to prove each and every theory.'

'Well, in that case Inspector, make yourself comfortable. The Queen has been learning magic from me for hundreds of years and I will need to list every spell I taught her.'

Many hours later he rose from the comfortable couch and made his way back to his office, where he found that the amount of time that he had spent in the woods was less than an hour.

'Oh, Lordy me, I couldn't live in that magic world for ever,' he said to Inspector Droove.

'Yeah, I know what you mean. Useful sometimes but would rather do without.'

'We need another expert to sift through these spells and make sure none of them could be used for killing someone.'

'You think the Queen has outwitted the Fairy Godmother?'

'No, but we have to prove she hasn't. Set someone on to finding another expert we can use.'

'I'm on it.'

Sitting down at his desk Solomon put his head in his hands and thought that he was getting nowhere fast with this case. The Queen had gone, and it seems she had the greatest motive of all the suspects. Had he let a murderer slip out of his grasp? He didn't think so but was that just wishful thinking? The woman had fooled a lot of people for many years and kept up the pretence of being the worse for drink. She had been expert at it. But there are also some anomalies in the shares bought by the person unknown. For now, he must focus on that. The forensic accounting team had found eight accounts in Infracom so far, that money has been transferred in relation to the purchasing of these shares. If it wasn't so serious, he might have a good laugh at the names of the accounts. Purl Loin, Ali Mynne, E.M. Bezzle, Sir Reptitious, Miss A. Propriate, I. Filtch, L.I.Berate. All variations on underhand dealing. But there the trail led to Upworld and there was still the problem with the Upworld banks. The paperwork had gone in to request information, but it was slow coming back. He knew that some of the Upworld banks, the older ones refused to acknowledge the Infraworld. With comments like, 'We don't believe in Fairies.' Well you soon will matey, thought Solomon.

Chapter 23

The transport hub was full of press. The arrival home of the Prentiss' was important news in Infraworld. Pixies all over the terminal, some with recording devises and cameras, some younger ones had taken the option of having a memory chip inserted. They could record and retain or delete every conversation they either had or over heard. This was something that the Prentiss brothers wished they had marketed, but it was an Upworld invention.

Travel in the Infraworld is very different to travel in the Upworld. Being a world of magic, this was one of the permitted uses. So, no long-haul flights for these souls. They just stepped into a car like vehicle and within seconds would reach their destination. This was the first time Esme and Gris had spent any time apart. They had trepidations about now living apart even with their attentive husbands. But the honeymoon had been fun, for both of them and they were now excited to see each other again. Two weeks, two whole weeks.

Richard and Stuart were happy to be home as well. Now the launch would be going ahead. The phone's adverts were everywhere, On the T.V. in the cinema, on bill boards, all over social media. It would be hard for any Fairy , Pixie, Goblins, Elf, Witch, Leprechaun or any other fantasy character to have missed it apart from the odd Hermit.

The Pixies were also there to get comments from Esme and Gris about the investigation. So many questions to ask and so many answers they probably wouldn't get. But being journalists, they had to try though. They would be sorely disappointed. The couples went from the hub to their own vehicle which took them to the Manor house. Baron Hardwick was the first person to visit. In fact, they would be staying with him until the houses they would be living in were furnished. Richard and Stuart had been advised to leave that to the girls, by Ella.

The houses situated in large gardens but next door to each other had been newly built. Every electronic device known to both Upworld and Infraworld had already been installed. Self-cleaning floors, thought controlled heating in each room, thought controlled lighting and entertainment systems. If it had been invented, it had been installed. The finishing touches had been put in place while the couples were away.

Bursting into the house Esme and Gris were surprised to see the parlour empty. Where was the Baron? They called and eventually he came to greet them from the green door, the servant's quarters.

'Whatever were you doing in there Dad?' asked Esme.

'Just having a spot of lunch with the boys and girls.' The Baron answered wiping his mouth and coming over for a kiss with his daughters. 'How was your holiday, did you have a fabulous time all of you? Tell me all about it and we can have some tea in the parlour.'

Richard and Stuart shook hands with the Baron but refrained from Taking tea. They had an appointment with D. C. I. Crumb. So, leaving their wives with the Baron they went off to Police headquarters.

'What is the latest news, Dad, about Mum?' Esme asked when they were settled with their tea.

'Oh, there is so much you don't know.' He said and proceeded to catch them up on all the events since their wedding. The Queen leaving, being the main topic of the conversation.

'She was never drunk? How wonderful is that?' Gris exclaimed at the news. 'And she had found her love. How nice. But the poor King.'

'The Inspector suspects that someone has been dealing with shares in your husband's company in a very underhand manner as well. Apparently, he is an Upworlder, from what I can deduce. He has been doing something very shady which is what the Inspector wants to talk to Richard and Stuart about. I hate to say this, but I'm not sure how far they are implicated in all this.'

'Shady? Whatever can they have done that is shady?' Gris asked.

'When they get back from speaking to the inspector you may have to ask that question of them. So, now tell me all about your holidays, Are the Islands nice? Should I go, do you think?'

It didn't take long to shift the girl's thoughts from any possibility of shady deals to the fun they had. And then to the thought that today they would see their new homes for the first time as married women. The Baron heard all about the holiday homes and the fun time they had, tinged with the sobering thought that the girls had missed each other's company.

'Well, it's good to know that you will be just next door to each other and be able to ride out together as well.'

The interview with the inspector was not quite so jolly.

'What can you tell me about the Upworlder who is buying shares in your company?'

'We know it is happening, but honestly can't tell you who he is.' Richard told him. 'We never knew his identity. He approached us some years ago and offered plans for a product that he said he had invented. We liked the concept and brought it out after doing our own development. We paid him for the invention outright and patented it in the company name. He didn't want to give his name and so was happy to forgo the ownership. He has brought several products to us in this way now.'

Stuart added. 'Yes, has been bringing us products for some time and we have been market leaders since then.'

'You hired him to do this?'

'No, he brought us the stuff and we paid him. A simple transaction. He doesn't even get the royalties. As he preferred to remain anonymous. We have secured a sale for our holding in the company which goes through in the next few days. After the launch of our latest product the share prices are rising, and the time is right.' Richard informed him.

'How many products have you brought out with the knowledge that the idea was stolen?' the Inspector asked them.

'Stolen? Whatever do you mean? We haven't stolen anything.' Richard and Stuart were shocked to have this accusation thrown at them.

'We have information that the Upworld company are investigating the theft of papers which detailed products very similar to yours. Industrial Espionage they called it.'

'No, we bought ideas from the inventor himself.' Richard stated. 'We've never done anything underhand, illegal or even immoral. They cannot possibly suspect us of espionage?'

'That is their thought process at the moment. For your own sakes it would be prudent to identify the person. For instance, how was he paid, you said it was a simple transaction? But which account did the money go into? I would be grateful for this information and if it can be tied in with the same account that the share purchases are from?'

'Well we will certainly look into it, but I am shocked at the thought. You need to speak to Don Money our finance Director. He is the only person we know who has met him. He may be able to give a description at least. He says they have had several conversations in the past so may be able to help.' Stuart advised him.

'Yes, I will need to speak to him. You will inform him that I want to see him?'

'Of course, he will be pleased to help.'

'Mean while you will look into your accounts and see if you can shed any light on who this may be?'

'Yes, I still can't believe it though. You think it's right? That he stole those designs?'

'Who can say? But thank you for your time. That is all for now.'

The D. C. I.s departure from the interview room left a bitter taste for the two brothers. They thought things were going so well, if it was found that the designs were stolen what would happen? Would they face prison? They had accepted at face value the input from this person and paid accordingly. But could they prove that they hadn't hired him to steal from the Upworld company? Everything was in place for the sale of the company. Would this delay it? It could lose them millions if that were to happen. More if they were accused of industrial espionage. But how did that stand with the two law systems?

'Oh, for the love of all things holy!' exclaimed Richard.

'So polite of you brother, I was thinking of much stronger expletives than that.' Stuart replied.

'We need to get to the lawyers and see what the implications are. They haven't thought of this in their calculations I'm sure.'

'Not in their offices though, it could get out.'

'Oh, so suspicious, but you're right we need them to come to the manor house.'

'I'll phone them.' Stuart said leaving the room.

'Yes, tell them we will meet them at the Hardwick Manor asap.'

Chapter 24

The King was also consulting his lawyers. He wanted to know the legal position of his marriage.

'Well, Sir, the Infraworld law is very clear on the dissolution of marriages. Her Majesty has in all effects deserted you and as such you are free to divorce at your will. We just need some signatures from her and we can start the ball rolling. So, to speak.'

'And what if I can't get any signatures from her?'

'There will be a period of seven years before the divorce can be finalised.'

'Seven years? Why so long?'

'Well the assumption would be that she had died, and our laws copy those of Upworld in this aspect.'

'But if I could get her to sign these papers you talk of? I can divorce straight away?

'Indeed, she needs to give her consent.'

'I don't think she will object but it's getting to her that's the problem.'

'Seven years will pass in a flash Sir.'

'Seven years of limbo. I don't think so. So, consent to agree to desertion is that the only grounds for divorce in such a case?'

'With the no fault policy, we have adopted for many hundreds of years that is the only way for divorce to come about in Infraworld. We did away with the contentious issues of finding fault for marriage breakdown many eons ago. Divorce is much more, shall we say, popular than it was. The fact that we are immortal means the average marriage could last hundreds of years and that is too much for some.'

'I see. Thank you I will have to find a way to see her.' As his lawyers left the King settled in his chair to think of how he could get to see the Queen, or ex-Queen. Maybe he would not have to find a way to go himself but could get the papers to her, but would she send them back? Why is nothing ever easy? He has yet to find out who that beauty was behind him at the wedding. 'I'll bet she comes from another story and I'll never see her again anyway.' He mused to himself.

'Why are you in such a hurry to get divorced?' Charles said as he entered the King's study.

'I just don't want to be living in a limbo hell for the next seven years.'

'Seven?'

'Unless I can get her to sign papers giving her consent to divorce.'

'Not an easy one, that.'

'I feel I need to speak to the Fairy Godmother.'

'She may be able to help, I suppose. Can she flit from story to story?'

'I don't know, usually one needs an escort but maybe she can use magic we know nothing off.'

'Worth asking, I would have thought.'

'Yes, me too. I wonder if she is too busy to come over, or I could go to her. I haven't been out of the palace in ages. I may go for a ride and see if I can hunt down her country home.'

'Didn't ever think I would be the produce of a broken home.'

'Not really that, we were together all your childhood.'

'Physically, yes but it is now obvious that Mother was not here in heart.'

'Oh God, are you going to go through some sort of mental anguish? I don't think I can cope with that.'

'Just feel a bit deflated, that's all. As I expect you do.'

'To be brutally honest I really don't know how I feel, apart from angry, but angry at whom? Just with the system we had at the time I think but I have to control it and so do you.'

'Brave face for the outside world?'

'That's the sort of thing. You have Ella you can discuss it with, I just have to rage at myself.'

'Oh God, don't let us get into a who is worse off battle. We are both sad that she had to go and have to live with it.'

'You're right, no point wallowing in misery, there is work to do. We need to find a way to recoup our financial losses from the wedding.'

'Exactly why I came to see you. Ella received this letter from the Prentiss brothers, they say they are willing to pay for the extra security incurred. It will just be pocket money for them, but it's a nice gesture I think.'

145

'If they are serious, that will help. I was just looking through the final plans for Parliament. Here, take a look.'

'Blimey that's a thick file, I need some peace and quiet to read through all this, better get on with it then.' Said Charles, getting up and Taking the file with him.

'Don't go losing that file now, it's the only one.' The King said with a smirk on his face.

'I'm a big boy now Daddy, I will look after it.' Charles smiled back.

As Charles left the room, he was greeted by the Fairy Godmother who had just arrived.

'Hello, my dear, I hope I find you well? If not a bit sad.'

'Indeed, we are all a bit sad at mother's departure, but I didn't expect to see you here today?'

'I had the distinct feeling that your father needs me.'

'Go on in, he is alone at the moment.'

The Fairy Godmother gave the door a cursory knock and entered the Kings office.

'You have need of my services.' She said upon entering.

'Fairy Godmother, how did you know?'

'I just do. You need me to flit into another story for you, to see Sophia. You have papers for her to sign?' The King was flabbergasted that the Fairy Godmother should know all this. 'Do you have spies in the palace? In my office?'

'No, but anything that involves Sophia instinctively alerts me. She and I have been so close for so many years, that I just know when something regarding her comes up.'

'Of course, you knew of her plans and kept them secret from us all that time.' The Kings resentful tone of voice showed how much he blamed her for the situation.

'As I would yours, Ella's, anyone who entrusted me with a secret in fact. I cannot ever divulge such knowledge without consent. I'm sorry if that hurts you but it is in my makeup and must always be so.'

'I do understand, but it is hard to come to terms with.' The King sighed.

'To business, you want a quick divorce. Sophia must sign some documents for this to happen?' I can take them to her and get then signed. Or I could take you to her for a visit, but I would not advise that.'

'No, I don't ever want to see her again, I still have to make myself hope for happiness for her, but she has left such a mess behind and I resent that. It may show if I was to see her. I can't let that happen.'

'Wise decision.'

'These are the documents she must sign, I can entrust them to your safe keeping?'

'Need you ask?'

'Trust is in short supply at the moment, I'm afraid.'

'I understand. I will look after the papers.' with that the Fairy Godmother rose from the chair and left the room.

Chapter 25.

She knew she was being followed and felt the presence as she left the palace. It was not the D. C. I's. Imps, but a much darker presence, more fearful. She had not felt such discomfort before and this being meant her harm, she knew it. She also realised that she knew who it was. The Upworlder she had been tutoring in the ancient languages. But why would he be tailing her? And what did he want of her that he couldn't just ask? She could not delve into his mind to find the answer, something else that worried her.   How had he been able to block her?

He obviously knew more magic than he had let on to her over the years. When he first came to her as a student of the ancient languages, he seemed very genuine and only interested in the history of the spells. Now though he had a menace about him. She feared him. He had powers and he was getting stronger.   She was afraid that he may unleash some awful power which could hurt the whole of Infraworld. What did he want? Why was Crumb interested in him as well? Something to do with the Prentiss brother's company. But What? She knew she had to find out but first she must take the trip to Sophia's story.

Lord Middlemass thought he had been so clever while tailing the Fairy Godmother and that she had not noticed him. Congratulating himself on his guile he knew he had to keep an eye on her. She knew his secret and she could expose him. He wondered if she had realised yet that she knew his secret, he thought not. But any sign that she may tie him into the marriage of the brothers and his involvement in their company would be very dangerous for him.

After all this hard work and so nearly at the end of his plan, he couldn't afford anything to go wrong before the sale of the Prentiss brother's controlling interest in the company They didn't know where he obtained the inventions, he had sold them in the past. They were so gullible and unworldly. They had believed his story from the first.

But he knew that he was very close to being found out in Upworld as the spy who had been stealing secret designs. He could not go back there in his present guise. He still had need of the Fairy Godmother to help him to change his appearance permanently, so he could go home as Lord Middlemass and restore his family pile. Live the life he believed he was destined to live. As a rich man. The money was in place.

When the sale went through, his holding would be sold as well. He had a large shareholding in that company and this would be transferred through the usual routes into his Upworld accounts. Thank God the wedding went ahead, and those brothers decided to sell out right now. If they had not got married, they would never have sold the company and he wouldn't have been able to anonymously sell his holding as well. That bitch of a Step Mother nearly put a stop to it. But she is gone now, and his plan was coming to fruition. Lord Middlemass was a wealthy man. But this one had to keep his secret and how could he trust her to do that?

Don money had informed D. C. I. Crumb of the name of the account he paid the invention sales into was in the name of Pearl Loin. He also had noticed that this same account was the one that had been used to purchase such a large holding in the company. And indeed, all dividends were paid into that account. This is all the information Don Money could find and it got the D. C. I. exactly nowhere.

He was coming up against brick walls every way he turned in this investigation. He was getting a lot of pressure from the Chief Constable and needed to get a result on the murder of the Wicked step mother. His gut feeling was that this Pearl Loin account holder was an important link, but how to find out who this being is? Even the Chief Constable was having difficulty with the Upworld banks. They were very reticent to give any information regarding the trail of money once it reached the Upworld.

He was however getting better results from his inquiries into the Industrial Espionage. The Upworld Secret Police were far more co-operative. Mainly because it would help them as well to find out more about the individual. Maybe the Chief Constable could lean on them to get the information from the banks. He needed to discuss this with someone and went to see the Fairy Godmother.

Chapter 26

'Oh, my good gracious. What a day! I'm so glad to be able to have a sit down.' Buttons walked in to his own apartment to find Dan already there making dinner.

'Wine?'

With a cheeky smile Buttons replied, 'Just a small whinge.'

Raising his eyes to the ceiling at the rubbish joke, Dan poured some red wine for his lover.

'What has made you so very exhausted then?'

'Ella's winter collection which she is showcasing in September.'

'For Fecks sake it's not even summer yet.'

'That's how it's done in the fashion world, my darling. She has really got a steam on with it and is working me to the bone.'

' AHHH' poor diddums?'

'No sympathy from you then?'

'The Prince is keeping me just as busy. I have to read these really confusing documents. Those plans of the King to turn us in to a democracy.'

'What's that when it's at home? I can't say I understand all these politics.'

'I don't really understand it all, but it means we all get to vote on laws and such like. I think.'

'That's a bit Upworldish isn't it?'

'I think that's where the idea came from. Ultimately it should take much of the work of the shoulders off royalty. They can fill their times opening things and visiting places. The Laws and such will be decided by Parliament.'

'Oh, I've read about those. Lots of stuffy old men cheering and jeering.'

'That's about it as far as I can see. Anyway, dinner's ready. Just got to wait for our visitor.'

'Oh God, I forgot I had invited her over. Mrs Qwell. Poor dear is at a bit of a loss now the Queen has done her moonlight flit.'

'There she is, shall I go?'

'Yeah, let her in, I'll just go have a quick wash to freshen up.'

Mrs Mary Qwell the ex-Private Personal Secretary to the Queen came in armed with two bottles of gin. It's well known amongst the staff that she has been giving away the Queen's stocks. Having finished winding up the Queens appointments and engagements she is wondering what to do with her time. She had been invited to dinner in many apartments in the block. Told the story to all who will listen, in fact you could say she has been dining out on the Queen's disappearance. Well-liked and a funny lady she has many stories to tell.

'So, when did you first know about the Queen's plans?' Dan asked her.

'I didn't know anything, my dear. That's one secret she kept from me. I knew all about her life but not that. I must say I was a bit miffed that she didn't tell me. I have had to go through her diary and cancel everything. Just as if she had died. Dreadful letters to write, I can tell you.'

'No-one it the palace knew she was about to bugger off?' Buttons asked.

'Nope, the Fairy Godmother was the only one who knew anything. But what do I do now? No work to do no boss to cater for? I'm getting very bored of it all. Thought I may write a book on Fairy tale etiquette.'

'How to act drunk and incapable and sod off to another world, under everyone's noses?' Dan scoffed.

'I would need to consult lawyers about that one,' she laughed. 'Any more news on the investigation?'

'I know that D. C. I. Crumb is looking for an Upworlder, not sure if he suspects him in the murder, but there are some weird going's on with the boy's business accounts.' Buttons told them. 'Ella has been talking about it and there is some sort of link there, I think. Apparently, it seemed important to this fella that the marriage went ahead. He may have killed the old bitch to make sure the wedding didn't get cancelled.'

'Intriguing! Maybe I should write a story about all that. Much more interesting than the drunk Queen.'

'Mary Qwell, you old mischief maker.'

'Need an income, my savings won't last long and who wants to employ an old weary secretary? Anyway, it may be fun.' she said with a coquettish shrug. 'Thanks boys, you have just given me a brilliant idea.'

Also having dinner were Esme, Gris and their respective husbands. Their discussion was much deeper, more nerve wracking.

'So, that's it in a nutshell.' Richard stated. 'We have no more idea who this Upworlder is than the Inspector.'

'But it was important to him that we got married and you sold your shares?' questioned Esme. 'Does he think this man murdered Mum?'

'That's the line he is Taking, and this man is in our world. Local, in this town. But there are so many Upworlders here now legally that it is a monstrous job to find out who he is.'

'But the money is being transferred to other accounts? Where then? Upworld?' Gris asked.

'Apparently, yes. The Inspector is having a right job getting the Upworld banks to give over any info. If they know at all.'

'Is there a way to identify him without the banks? How about the Fairy Godmother? Can't she find out?'

'She probably can, but can she tell him? She had to sign away her life to keep secrets, so she could practice magic. She told me once.' Esme piped in. 'By the way Gris, how is your house coming on? I haven't been round lately to look at what you've done?'

'Well we have the kitchen in, and I think the cook is very pleased with it. I sort of let her design it as she will be using it more than me. Catering standard, all stainless steel and easy to clean. Lots of storage and every conceivable utensil. I'd love to be getting in there but a bit worried about leaving Dad alone here.'

'He seems to be making himself at home in the servant's quarters, has all his meals in there and only comes out to go to his study.'

'Well at least he won't be lonely when we go. Comfortable as it is here, I really want to start my married life. None of this business is going to hold up the sale is it darling?' Gris asked her spouse.

'No, the sale will go ahead as planned and the day is getting close now. Very close. The new phone is selling well, and our share prices are climbing to new heights. As they level off, we will kick in the sale. Then my lovely I am all yours.'

'Yep, we can take early retirement and live the life of country gentlemen. And we will be in this new upper house the King has in mind when his democracy bill becomes law.' Richard added.

'Yes, I have been reading about the Upworld democracy and it looks quite a good system. All beings over a certain age will have a vote and they can decide who represents them in the two houses? Is that right?' Esme asked

'Well that's how they work it in some countries, sort of I think, and the King is trying to follow that model. He is furiously trying to get it finished now according to Ella.' Gris said.

'Maybe we should think of becoming politicians then, just in case you get fed up with us being around all the time.' Stuart said.

'Not likely, I want you home with me apart from the times you have to be in the Upper House.' Gris told him.

Esme agreed with that sentiment. Wholeheartedly. They both wanted their husbands home as much as possible, at least for now.

Chapter 27

Solomon Crumb settled at his own dining table for the first time in what seemed like ages. Philomena had insisted that he be home for their meal for once. She packed Polly off to bed as soon as she could, and Thom was out as usual.

'So, tell me all the latest.'

'How ever do I find out who this Upworlder is? He seems to be a key to open many secret boxes. I'm not sure yet if he is a prime suspect but he had a reason to want the marriage to go ahead. I have to go to the Golden door tomorrow and meet with someone from the banks.'

'Upworld? You're not going alone are you? I don't trust that lot.'

'No, I am to accompany the Chief Constable. I have never seen the other side of the door, apparently it's very beautiful up there. Glastonbury Tor.'

'Why is he going?'

'One of the Upworld banks want some information we hold on someone. Not our man, but we may be able to make them give us the information we need in exchange. Or they may be able to influence the other banks to be a bit more forthcoming.'

'So, when are you going to see the Fairy Godmother?'

'Probably best to leave it till I get some response from them, I may not have to disturb her. I have a feeling that any info she can have of use would be in her non-divulge files.'

'Humm, you can't ask her to tell you anything from those, It's more than her life's worth.'

'I know, but I'm sure she holds the answer. If I can find out who it is that is buying shares, and getting very rich in the process, another way I won't have to ask her awkward questions. Questions she can't answer.'

'You will be back in Infraworld tomorrow night, won't you? You don't have to stay there?'

'I have to travel to London and their transport is nowhere near as efficient as ours. So, it may be a couple of days.'

'What?'

'I'm sorry my love but I will be careful. And just because they are Upworlders, doesn't meant they will all be criminals. You watch too many films and read too many books from Upworld.'

Philomena bristled at the reference to her hobby of reading crime thrillers. 'Credit me with some intelligence Solomon. I do know the difference between fiction and fact. But don't forget I also read the newspapers from Upworld and probably have a greater understanding of the crime statistics up there than you have.'

'Sorry, I didn't mean to belittle you. I promise I will be very careful. But it is purely an exchange of information.

Nothing more. The Chief Constable is forever popping up there.'

'Why does he need you with him this time? He could get your information for you?'

'I want to go.'

'And you want me to pack a bag for you. And wait here for your safe return. And be quiet about it. And not worry. Anything else?'

'You could use some of your magic to keep me safe?'

'You know I have never used magic, Solomon.'

'Well, maybe just the once?'

Philomena blushed and looked away. Then smiling she looked back at her husband and said. 'Couldn't wait any longer for you, could I?'

At last, she had confirmed his lifelong suspicions. The first time she had admitted to him that she had used a love potion. He was flattered, amused and grateful that it had worked. He still loved her to pieces.

So, it was that the following day Solomon stood on the top of Glastonbury Tor. His first visit to Upworld. He knew that the Chief Constable and himself had to walk a long way before they found a rail station to get a train to London. It was a lovely day and he took a few moments to take in the country side. No doubt about it, this is a beautiful place. He could feel the pull of the door to Infraworld, but he needed to keep Walking. He thought he should feel frightened, but he felt at peace here. That peace faded as he moved away from the magic. His first time on a train was not very comfortable. He wondered why the Upworlders put up with such discomfort. Hard seats, being bounced about by the movement of the train, people everywhere Taking up more space than they should. The smells as well, some of them most unpleasant. Not an experience he was enjoying. Once they arrived in London, after a long journey he was bombarded by the claustrophobic feeling of being surrounded by hordes of people. Being dragged along with the crowds as they made their way to the station exit. A fearful taxi ride to the bank headquarters where they were greeted by and officious young man. He told them that the banks Governor would see then in due course. This of course was his way of playing mind games and was designed to make the two Goblins feel inferior. Well that wasn't going to work because they had plenty to occupy themselves with, discussing the case.

Eventually they were shown into the huge ornate office of the bank governor.

'Good afternoon gentlemen, I hope your journey was uneventful?'

'Indeed, some of it was quite pleasant, the walk from the Tor to the train station.' The Chief told him. Solomon hid a smile at the implied insult at the Upworld transport system.

'Well I am very grateful that you have taken the trouble to visit us here. I will not keep you any longer than I must. There is a person we believe is Taking refuge in your world that is of interest to us. This man has stolen a huge amount of cash in several daring bank robberies. Here are the details. We would greatly appreciate your help in locating him. Our Police have no jurisdiction in Infraworld and have stopped the search for him.'

The chief picked up the file and indicated to the D. C. I. to produce their file. He then nodded to Solomon to speak next.

'Of course, we will help if we can and will try to find your perpetrator. In return we need your help in ascertaining the identity of a man we have interest in. We have trailed his bank accounts all around the Infraworld but haven't been able to obtain any information regarding his accounts in Upworld. Your banks are most unhelpful in that regard. This man is suspected of murdering a prominent member of the Fairy tale society. We would also be most grateful for information which could lead to his identity even if it is just to eliminate him from our inquiries.'

The bank Governor looked decidedly put out. He thought he was able to access information from Infraworld without any consequences, but it seemed that there would be a price to pay after all.

'I will see what I can do. If he is not a customer of ours it may take some time. Usual contact method?'

'There are, I believe universal email links between the two worlds now, if you use this address the information will get to me. I will be able to pass any information we find of your defector. If you just send a test email now, I will then have your email to get that information to you much quicker.' Solomon told him with immense satisfaction. This would at last give him a direct contact with Upworld and save the weeks of waiting for replies to inquiries. Worth all the discomfort of the journey just for that.

The bank Governor typed Solomon's email address into his browser and pressed send. The phone in Solomon's pocket buzzed and with great aplomb he pulled it out and checked that the email had arrived. He also saved the address of the sender.

'Well I don't think there is much else we can do here at present, so we will leave you to your important work.' the Chief Constable told the man sitting in the biggest chair the two Goblins had ever seen. They took their leave.

'Well done Solomon, nice bit of tit for tat. Now shall we stay in London for the night or get out of this town?'

'If we head back towards Glastonbury and find somewhere to stay, we will be sure to be there at the right time for the door opening.' Solomon replied. Hoping to hell that the Chief agreed with that plan.

'Good thought, let's go, I hate this place. Full of miserable looking people.' They headed back to the train station for the first train out of London. To the transit hotel near the Golden door.

'What are your thoughts about this Upworlder? You think he killed the Wicked step mother?' The chief asked as the two Goblins settled in the hotel bar with a pint of good Fairy beer.

'I honestly don't know Sir, but he is of interest and may hold some information we need. I have no other leads. We do know that magic was used, and he has been studying it for a while. He has a connection with the Prentiss brothers. He wanted out of the tangle he found himself in and to do that he had to make sure they got married.'

'Because if they carried on with the company, they would want more inventions from him? The Fairy Godmother must know who he is'

'Exactly that, they would not have sold up and started their new life if they had not got married. And she can't tell us. Even then she would only know a name he told her which may not be truthful.'

'You have discounted the Queen?'

'Not entirely, but if she did kill that woman, we have lost her, there is no way we can get her back.'

'God, it's complicated isn't it?

'Yes, but I'm sure we are just missing one link to get to the truth. I believe this man holds that link. But who the hell is he?'

'Shame we can't just round up all the Upworlders and question them all.'

'Hardly democratic. What do you think of the King's plan for parliament?'

'Well it's going to be a mess, but he seems very keen on it. I do like the idea. Any thoughts of going into politics?'

'Oh, good grief no. You?'

'Thinking about it, but if he follows the English pattern, I won't have to, as retired Chief I'll be in the upper house. If you can solve this case, you stand a good chance of Taking my job.'

Solomon thought about this for a while and wondered if he wanted the job. He thought not.

Chapter 28

The Fairy Godmother prepared to make the trip to another story. She would keep her promise to the King and make her way to Sophia's home. There were other matters she must deal with while she was there also. Well at least this way she would be able to jettison the Upworlder who was still consistently shadowing her. He was constantly on her mind and on her tail. What could he want?

He had been a soothing presence when Taking lessons from her but now there was a malign aura to him. He wanted to do her harm, she knew it. She had to shake him off, so she could get to the portal gate. But he was hard to get away from. Even when she became invisible, he seemed to know where she was.

Everything was ready, and she only had to get to the portal. Does it matter? If he follows her to the portal? He may disrupt the journey. But even if he got through with her would that really matter? Normally, probably not, but she knew she had to go alone on this trek. Right then, off I go.

She set off from her country residence into the depths of the Enchanted wood, he was there, she could feel his evil presence. As she darted from place to place through the woods in decreasing circles to disguise her path. He was still there. She couldn't shake him off. She was getting close when her appointed time to pass through. That's the tree, she thought. I need to get to it. It stood there in all its majesty, this Oak tree. The gate to Sophia's world.

The Fairy Godmother approached the tree and walked around it once, twice, three times. Hoping to confuse the malignant spirit. When she though he was on the far side of the tree she launched herself at it and jumped inside. Immediately she felt the power of the tree transporting her. She also felt release from the evil awaiting her on her return. With a great sigh of relief, she proceeded to Sophia's house.

'Fairy Godmother, what brings you here?'

'My dear, not only did I want to see that you are alright, but I bring a message from the King.'

Sophia invited the Fairy Godmother into her home. A small wooden cabin set in a perfect glade. A picture book babbling brook running through the land. Pens for goats, and sheep. A horse wandering close by. Inside the cabin was much larger than appeared from outside. The kitchen area set to one side and a comfortable lounging area, where she was now sitting. It was everything an Ex-Queen could want. Sophia looked young and happy.

'What is it that the King wants to say?' Sophia asked.

'I have come with a message from him, he asks if you would be so kind as to sign these papers. It will release him from your marriage.'

'Didn't waste much time, did he?'

'Were you thinking of coming back?

'Good God, no.'

'Well, you can't have it both ways, can you? He will get a divorce anyway but will have to wait.'

'Until I am considered dead?'

'Yes, apparently that is so.'

'Well, I suppose it will free me as well. I wouldn't want him to wait. Is there someone he has in mind to replace me?'

'I don't know but I doubt it, not yet anyway. He is a stickler for convention and law. He would be unlikely to pursue any relationship while still in a marriage, however broken and dead it may be.'

'That's true. He is a good man, just not the one for me.'

'Where is Raphael?'

'Out with his dogs, He will be back soon. Can you stay for a while?'

'I can, but not for long. I have unfinished business to deal with.'

'How is the investigation going?'

The Fairy Godmother brought Sophia up to date with all the progress of the case that she knew. She also told her of the now malign presence that surrounded Lord Middlemass. Sophia had studied with him at the Fairy Godmother's town house. She had thought him quite pleasant for an Upworlder. The fact that he had turned nasty came as a surprise to her.

'He obviously thinks you know something that could harm his plans. If he is the person buying all those shares? Could he really be the one who killed the bitch?'

'That's always possible, I suppose. He seems to know more magic than he let on to us. All those years studying the ancient language? For what reason? I can't understand why I didn't question it before now. Why would he want to know all that? Has he found a way to use the Infraworld magic in the Upworld? He could be very dangerous if that is the case. I have been thinking all these things out and I really need to talk to him. But I fell such malevolence from him. It frightens me.'

'And you have no protection spells to use?'

'For some reason they don't seem to be powerful enough.'

'Oh, do be careful, he is becoming more of a danger all the time by the sounds of it.   Ah, I hear the dogs, Raphael will be here any moment. Where are those papers to sign, let's at least get that out of the way? I will conjure up some food for us all.'

As if my magic, which of course it was, there appeared a feast of wholesome food on the table. Fresh baked bread, and a big pot of stew. It was delicious and once replete The Fairy Godmother took her leave of the loving couple. She had a wander about in the woods enjoying the peace and freedom in this happy place. When she entered another glade, which seemed to be perfection to her, she settled down for a while by a big tree to enjoy the peace and quiet. This is a wonderful place she thought to herself. A perfect retirement spot.

After a while she roused and braced herself to go back
to the darkness and fear of her home world.

'Ah, there you are Fairy Godmother,' a voice she
knew so well, interrupted her thoughts as she rested
again after travelling through the portal.

'My dear Baron, whatever are you doing so far in the
Enchanted Woods?'

'Well, to be honest, I am lost. I'm so glad I came
across you Taking a nap by that tree, I'm' not sure of the
way home.'

'We shall walk together, shall we? How are you
getting on my dear? I hope you are not being overrun
by exuberant young people?'

'Not at all, the girls are out most of the time
furnishing their respective houses. Spending pots of
money, which they so love to do. They are in seventh
heaven. There is a mist of happiness around the Manor,
something it has not felt in an age.'

'You're not getting lonely, are you?'

'I do spend an inordinate amount of time in the
servant's hall, they have become more like friends and
family and are a great comfort to me.'

'That's good. I'm glad they are of comfort to you. And
Rose, how is she doing without her Mistress giving
orders here there and everywhere?'

'Rose felt a bit lost at first, but she has been making
herself useful to the girls and myself. She was worried
that there would not be a job for her, but I couldn't

chuck her out, could I? She is such a gentle person, how she managed Madeline all those years amazes me.'

'A woman of many talents. Here you are, the path to your home. And that way to mine.'

'Oh, I wasn't that far away then? Silly me, to get lost so close to home.'

'Never underestimate the Enchanted Woods, my dear.'

'Good day to you Fairy Godmother.'

'Good day Baron.'

As they parted company, she felt again the heavy darkness surround her. He's back, she thought. As she made her way to the palace.

Chapter 29

The report from the Imps made disturbing reading. Solomon wondered why this Uplander was so interested in The Fairy Godmother. He seemed to spend all his time tracking her movements. The Imps were puzzled as well. They had split up and some followed the Fairy and some the Upworlder. But they kept meeting up. Very strange.

'Time to have a word with her' he told Droove. The very speaking of his thoughts made his phone ting, The Fairy Godmother said. 'D. C. I. Crumb, I think you wish to see me?'

'Yes, Ma-am where would be best to find you?'

'I'm in the woods, I'll see you here as soon as you like. Oh, and yes, please do bring your Inspector with you.'

'Thank you, Ma-am, we are on our way.'

'I didn't hear you ask if I could come?'

'Magic Droove, magic.'

The two policemen left the building and in minutes were in the Enchanted Woods facing the shrub entrance of the Fairy Godmother's country home. They felt the presence of the Upworlder nearby.

'You need to know more of my stalker? He is an Upworlder named Lord Middlemass and for many years I have been teaching him the ancient language. I had thought it was merely a hobby for him but have come to suspect that he has deeper motives. He worries me.'

'What can you tell us about him?' D. C. I. Crumb asked.

'I think he is implicated in the financial affairs of Infracom. The company has been at the forefront of communications for a long while and apparently their inventions were stolen from the Upworld company?'

'I won't ask how you know this information Ma-am, you have your methods. Have you ever thought of joining the police force?' Droove asked her.

'Unfortunately, unless the danger is to me alone, I cannot divulge any more, Inspector. Suffice to say that this man worries me, and I feel unsafe with him following me. I think he means to do me harm and I now know he has more magic than I first imagined.'

'You think he is the person we have been searching for? But would he have wanted the wedding to go ahead, I would have thought that putting a stop to it would have been more productive for him,' Droove mused.

'Quite the contrary, Droove, apparently he wanted to get out of the arrangement. The feeling being that he was about to be exposed by the Upworld company. So knowing that the Prentiss Brothers were going to sell up and leave upon marriage, means he would want the wedding to happen. So, he is even more suspect.' Solomon told him.

'I think you are right D. C. I. Crumb. He must have been the person that killed Madeline. He has the magic, he can perform the spell that killed her. He had me fooled as only an Upworlder with magic can do.'

'Which begs the question of how to interview him? If he thinks we are on to him, he can magic his way out of getting arrested. We are Goblins and although we have enormous strength will we be able to hold an Upworlder who can magic himself out of any situation?'

'That is something I have been puzzling about as well. He is elusive when he wants to be.'

'How can we help protect you? If he has so much magic, there isn't much help we can be.'

'Just keep your Imps on him so you know where he is, that's about all we can do now. He may show himself. Especially now that he has seen you arrive here.'

'Because he thinks you are about to denounce him? As, indeed you just have? A dangerous move if I may say so.' Solomon said.

'Yes, but I felt it necessary as it was becoming oppressive and I cannot concentrate on my important work with him hanging around. I have protection while I am here, he cannot enter without an invitation, which I have no intention of extending. I am vulnerable when travelling though.'

'Can you stay inside the confines of your home here for a while? Until we can figure out a way to get to him?' Droove asked.

'I think I must.' She answered.

'We will leave the Imps watching him and see if we can find a way to get him in to see us.'

As they left the shrub D. C. I. Crumb stopped by the car and spoke loudly to Inspector Droove.

'Silly old bat, can't see what she's worried about, he's an Upworlder after all, how can he have power over the Fairy Godmother in her own realm? She could zap him in an instant if she so wished.'

Catching the very slight wink from his D. C. I. Inspector Droove answered. 'Perhaps the old girl's losing it? Anyway, he's of no interest to us. What a waste of time all that was.'

'Yeah, let's get back. I'd like to talk to him, just to eliminate him from the inquiry, let's face it all he did was sell some inventions to Infracom. Not any of our business where he got them from.'

Lord Middlemass listened to this exchange. And wondered if he was in fact becoming paranoid. Perhaps they were as stupid as he first suspected. The Infraworld Police force had never had to deal with a murder before. They weren't experienced in such crimes. He reasoned to himself. He was tired and would dearly love to be able to rest. All this stalking of the only person who could know the extent of his involvement was taking its toll on him.

Chapter 30

The two brothers were worried that there would be repercussions from the revelations from D. C. I. Crumb. What if it was true and the Upworlder had stolen the designs and was caught? What if he said that they had asked him to get the blueprints for them? He could do, to try and mitigate his crime. Should they come clean and let the Upworld company know? What would happen to them if they did?

Richard and Stuart were in a meeting with their lawyers. They had explained the suspicions of the police. Concerned that they would face charges of fraud and business theft they wanted to know the implications. Richard was doing the talking while Stuart took notes

'You bought these items in good faith? Then there should be no repercussions.' The laws of Upworld have no jurisdiction in Infraworld,' The Lawyer told them

'But, how do we prove that we didn't know they were stolen?'

'There lies the rub, there would be no way to prove that. It would be just your word against his if they came to court.'

'But what could we be charged with? Industrial espionage? As the police said? And would the company be held responsible or us personally?'

'The company would be held responsible and would face a large fine. But as the company is about to change hands they may come after yourselves. Don't forget it is only suspicions at present. They don't know if those designs were stolen or who might have taken them. It could be all coincidental.'

'That would be your argument?'

'If action was taken against you, they would have to have more to go on than suspicions of possible theft. They would have to find the perpetrator and then he or she would also need to implicate you. As far as we can see the persons unknown that may have committed these crimes has not been identified. You only have a tenuous interaction with your source. Please put your minds at rest until the Upworld company discovers who their spy may be. And even then, they would have to prove he sold their designs to you.'

'Well, I feel a bit more comfortable now. Even if they do find out that our source is their thief, would they be able to bring action against us here from Upworld?'

'It is unlikely they will be able to take such action. As I said the laws of Upworld are still separate from ours and only a few cross the divide. This one is not yet on the list for interaction. I have been in touch with a trusted Upworld lawyer friend who has told me that even now there are only suspicions. They cannot be sure that there had been any design theft carried out. They also have no conception of who may have done it. Please put your minds at rest, they need so much more than suspicions to go on.'

'So, you think the D. C. I. was just trying to scare us? Just phishing for any information, we may have?' Richard asked.

'Indeed, I am sure of it. He is floundering in the dark in regard to finding the perpetrator of the murder and is just looking for connections, so he can arrest someone. He has got nowhere with his investigations so far and is casting his net further afield. He is under pressure to come to a conclusion. He is a good detective and will find who is responsible. He may well be on the right track, but his main focus is finding the murderer not any subsidiary anomalies he may come across.'

'Well, thank God for that. It looks like we can relax little brother. We are not facing Upworld prison.' Richard sighed.

'Thank you for making the trip to see us here today. You have put our minds at some rest.'

The lawyers left the brothers and very soon Esme and Gris came into the room.

'All ok? They left smiling, so we presume that the worry was exaggerated?'

'We think so, you won't be losing your husbands to prison just yet.' Stuart told them.   'How about some lunch to celebrate. Where's your Dad? We could take him out to the pub if you like.' Richard added.

'Oh, he's gone for a ramble in the woods. He'll be ages yet so don't let's wait for him.'
Gris said.

'Yes, he has taken to going for long walks and often meets up with the Fairy Godmother. I wonder if she is counselling him. He seems much happier lately.' Esme added. 'She is a bit of a wonder woman, isn't she? Perhaps she's put a happy spell on him.'

'OK, lunch then we need to pop to the houses to make sure the work is being done properly. Gris told them. 'My bathroom is going in today.'
Obviously, the houses were the girls biggest concern at the moment and they wanted to move in as soon as possible. They were unaware of the depth of the turmoil their husbands had been going through.

Chapter 31

D. C. I. Crumb's phone tinged. A voice told him that a
certain Lord Middlemass had been seen again following
the Fairy Godmother. She was in the Enchanted Woods
gathering herbs. He was just watching her. It didn't
appear that she was in any danger.

'Droove, come with me, and bring back up.' He
ordered as the made his way through the incident
room.

In the car on their way to the woods Crumb told Droove
what he learned. There were five cars full of uniformed
officers following them. No sirens though, they didn't
want to warn their prey of their arrival yet. They pulled
up and Crumb told the assembled officers to spread out
and begin to search wherever the Imps directed them.

'Don't forget the Imps know these woods intimately
and were the last to see the Fairy Godmother'.

The search parties set out, under direction of the
Imps. Very soon they came to a clearing where they saw
the Fairy Godmother. Crumb had the officers surround
the clearing as quietly as they could in the hope that
they would be able to catch the Upworlder in the circle.
Once in position they were told to stand and wait.
Crumb wanted to make sure he would be able to detain
the Upworlder. He needed to talk with him. Crumb was
still not convinced that this man had killed the Wicked

step mother, but he really had to get to him. He knew
that the Fairy Godmother was in danger as this man
would have seen the police visit her. He would know
that she had informed the police of his identity. She
was in great danger as now under Fairy law he was
entitled to take his revenge on her if indeed he was the
perpetrator.

As Crumb watched he saw a figure emerge from the
woods into the clearing. Not his quarry but Baron
Hardwick. The Baron meandered over to the Fairy
Godmother and they conversed. Too far away for the D.
C. I. to hear what they were saying. No sooner had the
Baron reached her side than Crumb was alerted to
movement from another part of the circle.

'That's him. Our Man.' He directed his men to slowly
approach from all directions until they were just visible
surrounding the clearing.

'You denounced me, to the police.' He heard the
Upworlder say to the Fairy Godmother.

'Yes, and now I suspect you have come to take your
revenge. Are you going to use your black magic on the
Baron as well? He will be able to identify you.'
Lord Middlemass lifted an arm in which he held an
ancient wand. He pointed this at the two fairies. 'You
know I would if I could. I have the power now through
your teachings. I can reduce you both to a pile of ashes
and leave your cursed Fairy souls to hang about here
forever. You are a wicked woman and you need
dispatching before you can do further harm.'

'As you can see the police are all about you, you will not get away. Your own soul will live in hell for ever and a day. It is permitted that you kill me for denouncing you, but you will have to dispose of all these fairies, Goblins and Imps as well. You may have the power, but do you have the courage to face that? I think not. You are nothing. Your ancient book of spells and the language I taught you will not save you from the punishment you are going to receive.'

'I did nothing to warrant punishment from the Infraworld. You know that very well.'

As the police moved in closer to try to overpower the man, Crumb gave the order and twelve officers rushed to the man, they overpowered him with ease. Pinned his arms to his sides and pulled him to the ground.

Crumb thought that the operation was too easy and why hadn't this man used the purported powers he had? Why was he just giving in without a fight? He allowed the Goblins to secure him in restraints. This didn't make sense. He should by rights have extracted revenge on the Fairy Godmother. What was she saying, why would he have to kill the Baron? What was the woman talking about? She had been goading him into action.

As the Goblins lifted the man to his feet Crumb approached him. 'Lord Middlemass? Would you be good enough to explain this little scene to us?'

'My pleasure inspector. The Fairy Godmother has lured you all here to arrest me. She hopes you will then charge me with the murder of the Wicked step mother.

She let you know that if I was the perpetrator of that crime and she told you that information, I would then have the right to kill her. Yes?'

Crumb nodded. He looked at Droove and indicated that he should get his officers to surround the Fairy Godmother and the Baron. Some instinct told him to secure their safety. He hoped a circle of Imps and Goblins would be enough.

'She knows I cannot extract any such revenge, because I did not commit the crime, she is accusing me of. I came here today to confirm my suspicions.'

'Suspicions? What would you know of suspicions?' The Fairy Godmother scoffed.

'Detective Chief Inspector Crumb, the murderer is indeed in this clearing today, in fact both of them are.' The man said.

'You really expect us to believe that?' Droove asked.

'Ask yourself why I didn't just throw a magic spell on the Fairy Godmother as soon as I saw her today? Why did I wait until I was surrounded by police? If I was the guilty party, I could have thrown a spell on her at any time since she talked to you. You, yourself told her to stay within the confines of her home. But here she is in a clearing out in the woods.'

'Putting herself in danger, to lure you out?' Droove asked.

'Exactly, so you could arrest me.'

Crumb indicated to Droove to tighten the cordon around the two fairies. At the same time, he realised that he knew the answer to the conundrum. As he undid the restraints holding the Upworlder he said in a very loud order. 'Arrest those two. NOW!'

Before the Fairy Godmother could raise a hand to cast a spell she was restrained. She was powerless momentarily as she had been caught out in a lie and this weakened her.

'Yes, we got rid of the harridan that has made my life an utter misery for centuries. We have waited a long time for my freedom.' Baron Hardwick said. With tears in his eyes.

'Shut up you fool.' The Fairy Godmother demanded of the Baron. 'He is under a great strain Inspector. He doesn't know what he is saying. You know me Inspector Crumb. Are you really going to believe the words of an Upworlder over my own?' How could you believe his utterances? His lies.'

'You, Fairy Godmother are weakening your own powers with every lie you tell. And I am Detective-Chief-Inspector-Crumb, for your information'
'Take them away, both of them' Crumb ordered.

Diana Bettinson Author. If you like this book please feel free to write a short review on my Amazon page and tell all your friends. I have some other books that may also interest you and more to come. So watch this space

I can be found at:

dianabettionson@hotmail.com

https://www.facebook.com/Dbettinson

@Dibett on twitter.

https://dianabettinson.wordpress.com/

In a scrap yard awaiting certain death. Gari an old broken rotting mini cooper is saved and brought to a nice warm barn to be restored. While he is there he tells his life story to the other vehicles in the barn. During his happy times and his sad times from the brand-new car rolling out of the factory, his gradual decline in old age. Meeting the people who drove him during all this time, their lives and how they interact with his. Will he ever meet any of them again?

When Paula's husband of thirty-two years dies, suddenly, she wonders if she can cope. After a lifetime of being told what to do and how to live her life, how will she carry on? Will she find love again, and will she want it? This is a story of love, betrayal, control and manipulation.

Mary Qwell

Walking Trees

Mary Qwell

23012644R00113

Printed in Great Britain
by Amazon